THE DREAMER

The East Harlem School
309 E. 103rd St.
New York, NY 10029

THE DR

BY PAM MUÑOZ RYAN

SCHOLASTIC PR

EAMER

DRAWINGS BY PETER SÍS

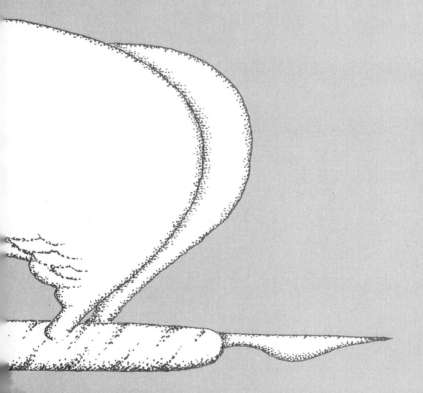

ESS • NEW YORK

To my reader,

This book is for you.

Wander into that infinite space

between soul and star.

I am waiting for you there.

~PMR

To our family house Nerudova 19 Prague

~PS

"LOOK AROUND —

THERE'S ONLY ONE THING OF DANGER

FOR YOU HERE . . ."

~*Pablo Neruda*

I am poetry,

waiting to seize the poet.

I ask the questions

for which all answers

exist.

I choose no one.

I choose every one.

Come closer . . .

. . . if you dare.

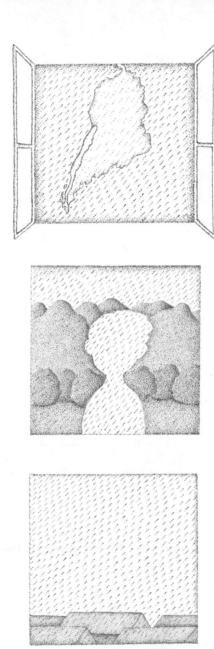

RAIN

ON A CONTINENT OF MANY SONGS, in a country shaped like the arm of a tall *guitarrista*, the rain drummed down on the town of Temuco.

Neftalí Reyes sat in his bed, propped up by pillows, and stared at the schoolwork in front of him. His teacher called it simple addition, but it was never simple for him. How he wished the numbers would disappear! He squeezed his eyes closed and then opened them.

The twos and threes lifted from the page and waved for the others to join them. The fives and sevens sprang upward, and finally, after much prodding, the fours, ones, and sixes came along. But the nines and zeros would not budge, so the others left them. They held hands in a long procession of tiny figures, flew across the room, and escaped through the window crack. Neftalí closed the book and smiled.

He certainly could not be expected to finish his homework with only the lazy zeros and nines lolling on the page.

He slowly stepped out of bed and to the window, leaning his forehead against the pane and gazing into the backyard. He knew that he should rest in order to recuperate from his illness. He knew that when he wasn't resting, he should catch up on his studies. But there were so many distractions.

Outside, the winter world was gray and sodden. The earth turned to mud, and a small stream flowed through a hole in the ramshackle fence. At the moment, no one lived next door. Still, Neftalí always imagined a friend on the other side, waiting for him – someone who might enjoy watching flotsam drift downriver, who collected twisted sticks, liked to read, and was *not* good at mathematics, either.

He heard footsteps. Was it Father?

He had been away, working on the railroad for a week, and was due home today. Neftalí's heart pounded and his round brown eyes grew large with panic.

The footsteps came closer.

Clump.

Clump.

Clump.

Clump.

Neftalí reached up and smoothed his thick black hair. Was it out of place? He held up his hands and looked at his thin fingers. Were they clean enough?

The idea of having to confront Father made

his arms tingle and his skin feel as if it were shrink-
ing. He took a deep breath and held it.

The footsteps passed his room and continued down the hall.

Neftalí exhaled.

It must have been Mamadre, his stepmother,
in her wooden-heeled shoes. He listened until he
was sure that no one was near, then he turned to
the window again.

Raindrops strummed across the zinc roof.
Water mysteriously trilled above him, worming
its way indoors. Weepy puddles dripped from
the ceiling, filling the pots that had been poised
to catch them.

plip – plip

plop

bloop, bloop, bloop

oip, oip, oip, oip

plip – plip

plip – plip

plop

tin,

tin,

tin,

tin,

tin

plop

plip – plip

bloop, bloop, bloop

oip, oip, oip, oip

tin,

tin,

tin,

tin,

tin

plip – plip

plip – plip

plop

As Neftalí listened to the piano of wet notes, he looked up at the Andes mountains, hovering like a white-robed choir. He looked out at the river Cautín, pattering through the forest. He closed his eyes and wondered what lay beyond, past the places of Labranza, Boroa, and Ranquilco, where the sea plucked at the rugged land.

The window opened. A carpet of rain swept in and carried Neftalí to the distant ocean he had only seen in books. There, he was the captain of a ship, its prow slicing through the blue. Salt water sprayed his cheeks. His clothes fluttered against his body. He gripped the mast, looking back on his country, Chile.

Neftalí? Who spoons the water

from the cloud to the snowcap to the river

and feeds it to the hungry ocean?

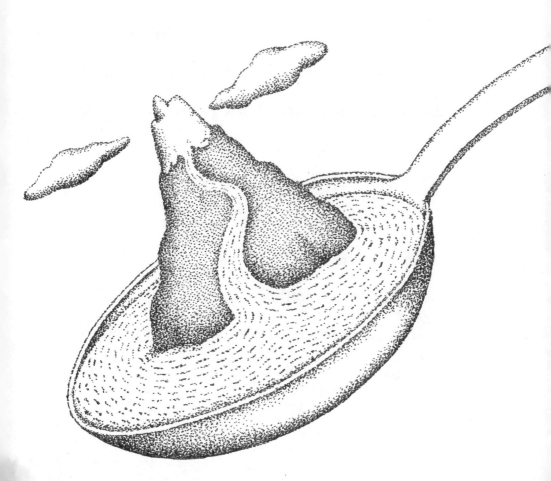

The screech of a conductor's whistle snapped Neftalí to attention. He jerked around.

Father's body filled the doorway.

Neftalí shuddered.

"Stop that incessant daydreaming!" The white tip of Father's yellow beard quivered as he clenched and unclenched his narrow jaw. "And *why* are you out of bed?"

Neftalí averted his eyes.

"Do you want to be a skinny weakling forever and amount to nothing?"

"N-n-n-no, Father," stammered Neftalí.

"Your mother was the same, scribbling on bits of paper, her mind always in another world."

Neftalí rubbed his temples. He had never known his mother. She had died two months after he was born. Was Father right? Could daydreaming make you weak? Had it made his mother so weak that she had died?

Mamadre hurried into the room.

Father pointed at her. "You need to watch him more closely. He must stay in bed or he will never get stronger." As he bounded from the doorway, the floor shook.

Mamadre took Neftalí's hand, gently helped him into bed, and tucked the blankets around him. "Your mother did not die from her imagination," she whispered. "It was a fever. And look at me. I am small and many say much too thin. I may not appear big and strong on the outside, but I am perfectly capable on the inside . . . just like you." She stroked his head. "I know it is hard to spend so many days in bed."

"I f-f-feel . . . f-f-fine," said Neftalí, reaching up to touch her black hair, which was pulled into a tight bun at the back of her neck.

"Just one more day," said Mamadre. "I will read to you to help pass the time."

Within the lull of Mamadre's soothing voice, Neftalí lost himself in the legends of swashbucklers and giants. There, his painful shyness stayed in the back of his mind. There, he could not be called "Shinbone" because of his thin and sickly body, or chosen last for a street game by the neighborhood boys.

Between the pages, he forgot that he stuttered when he spoke. He saw himself healthy and strong like his older brother, Rodolfo; cheerful like his little sister, Laurita; and confident and intelligent like his uncle Orlando, who owned the local newspaper. While the pages turned, he even dared to imagine himself with a friend.

After Mamadre finished reading and slipped away, Neftalí studied the cracks in the ceiling. They looked like roads on a map, and he wondered to which country they belonged.

He sighed. It had not mattered one bit what Father had said about daydreaming. Neftalí could not stop.

Every curious detail of his life taunted him. His mind wandered:

To the monster storm raging outside, which startled the roof. To the distant rumble of the dragon volcano, Mount Llaima, which made the floors hiccup. To the makeshift walls of his timid house, trembling and cowering from the roar of passing trains. To the haphazard design of the room with incomplete stairs, which might have led to a castle on another floor, but had long been deserted in the middle of construction.

Neftalí? To which mystical land

does an unfinished staircase lead?

The next day, Mamadre was far more watchful, and Neftalí could not escape from his bed. Instead, he begged Laurita to be his ambassador at the window.

"T-t-t-tell me all that you can s-see. Please. *¿Porfa?*"

Laurita nodded. She was only four and too short to see out. She pushed a chair to the window and climbed onto the seat. Then she leaned forward. Her round black eyes, heavy lashes, and sleek hair made her look like a little bird perched at the sill. "I see rain . . . bumpy sky . . . wet leaves . . . one boot missing the other . . . muddy puddles . . . *un perro callejero* . . . "

"T-t-tell me about the stray dog," said Neftalí. "What color is it?"

"It is so wet, I cannot say. Maybe brown. Maybe black," said Laurita.

"T-t-tell me about the boot that is m-m-missing the other."

"It has no shoestrings. It looks lonely."

"Tomorrow, when I am allowed up, I will rescue it and add it to my c-c-collections."

"But you already have so many rocks and sticks and nests. And the boot will be so dirty," said Laurita. "And you do not know where it has been. Or who has worn it."

"That is true," said Neftalí. "B-b-but I

will clean it. Maybe it belonged to a stonemason, and by owning it, I will receive his strength. Or maybe it belonged to a b-b-baker, and once I run my hands over the leather, I will know how to make b-bread."

Laurita giggled. "You are silly, Neftalí."

Just then, Mamadre appeared in the doorway. "Laurita, Valeria is here to play with you. And, Neftalí, you need a nap or you will not be able to go back to school tomorrow." She came into the room, kissed his forehead, and pulled the blanket up to his chin. "You look fine on the outside, my son. How do you feel on the inside?"

"Not tired. P-p-please, Mamadre, may I read for a while?"

"That is what I deserve for teaching you before you even started school." Mamadre nodded and smiled as she left the room. "One story."

Neftalí grabbed a book from the bedside table. Even though he did not know all of the words, he read the ones he knew. He loved the rhythm of certain words, and when he came to one of his favorites, he read it over and over again: *locomotive, locomotive, locomotive.* In his mind, it did not get stuck. He heard the word as if he had said it out loud – perfectly.

Neftalí climbed out of bed, retrieved a

pencil and paper, and copied the word.

LOCOMOTIVE

He folded the paper into a small square and put it in a dresser drawer already crammed with other words he'd written on tiny, doubled-over pieces of paper. Then he crawled into bed.

Father's question from yesterday found its way into his thoughts. *Do you want to be a skinny weakling forever and amount to nothing?*

The words in the drawer shuffled. The drawer opened. The small pieces of paper floated into the room and arranged and rearranged themselves into curious patterns above his head.

CHOCOLATE OREGANO

IGUANA

TERRIBLE

LOCOMOTIVE

Neftalí sat up, rubbed his eyes, and looked around the room. The words were no longer there. He slid from the bed, tiptoed to the drawer, and opened it.

All of the words were sleeping.

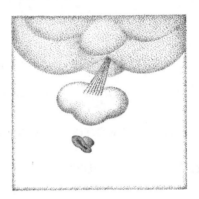

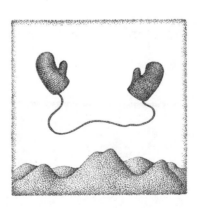

WIND

"LAH, LAH, LAH, LAH, LAH, LAH, lah, lah, laaaaaah . . ."

Neftalí awoke to Rodolfo, singing scales. Usually, he loved Rodolfo's voice, but not this morning. Father thought singing was a disruption. If Father was upset, he could easily withdraw a permission he had already granted. Would he still let Neftalí go to school today? Neftalí sprang from his bed, dressed, and ran to Rodolfo's room.

His big brother stood in front of the dresser, his dark hair disheveled, hands clasped at his chest, and his short muscular body standing as tall as he could make it. His tongue flapped the notes: "Lah, lah, lah, lah, lah, lah, lah, lah, laaaaaah . . ."

"R-r-rodolfo." Neftalí put one finger over his mouth as a warning. But it was too late.

Father's voice boomed through the house. "Rodolfo! Stop that useless noise at once!"

Rodolfo rolled his eyes, grabbed his jacket, and hurried past Neftalí.

Neftalí sighed, imagining the lecture to

come. He pinched his cheeks to make them look healthier, then followed Rodolfo to the kitchen.

When he arrived, the family was already seated. Rodolfo looked intently at his food and avoided Father's eyes. Mamadre passed Laurita the fig jam for her bread. Neftalí pulled out his chair and quietly sat down. Maybe there would not be a confrontation.

"Rodolfo, on the days I have been home the last month, all I have heard is your singing," Father lectured. "If you have so much extra time, you should spend it on your studies."

"But . . ." Rodolfo began, his eyes darting from Father to Mamadre.

Quietly, Mamadre nodded and said, "You must tell him."

Rodolfo took a deep breath and looked at Father. "I . . . I am rehearsing for a performance at school. And . . ."

Father leaned forward. "And . . . what?"

"My teacher and the headmaster say . . . that if I study music, I might be able to get a scholarship to the conservatory."

Father set down his fork. "I promise you that no son of mine will go to a music conservatory."

Rodolfo protested. "But . . . but they . . ."

Father slammed his fist on the table. Startled, Rodolfo jumped. Neftalí slid down in his chair. Laurita reached for Mamadre's hand.

"José," said Mamadre. "They think Rodolfo shows great promise."

"He is fifteen years old. In a few years he will be on his own. This diversion will serve him no purpose nor assure him a job." Father picked up his fork and shook it at Rodolfo. "I will not allow you to suffer my fate. For years I was a poor laborer, wandering from town to town to find work. . . ."

Neftalí and Rodolfo exchanged looks and their shoulders sagged. They had heard this story many times before.

"I struggled to put food on the table and

to save money," continued Father. "Finally, the railroad position came along and served me and this family very well. But it is no life for you. It is time to get serious about your future. You will study business or medicine. That is what I would have done if given the chance. There will be no more wasting time on music." He turned to Mamadre. "Send a note to his teacher."

Rodolfo closed his eyes. When he opened them, his lashes were wet.

Neftalí looked down at his plate. He did not want to make it worse for Rodolfo by staring at him.

"Now finish your breakfast so that you can

walk Neftalí to school. And make sure he arrives before the bell. We have already had one letter about his tardiness this year."

"It is not my fault if he wants to stop and collect every stupid thing," muttered Rodolfo.

"Make sure that he does not," said Father. "His mind needs to be filled with facts and figures, just like yours. Or he will always be a fanatic. And make certain he stays warm so he does not get sick again."

Neftalí looked from Rodolfo to Father. Could they not see him sitting there? He wished he had the courage to tell Father that he did not collect every stupid thing. He collected important things. And was Father right? Was he a fanatic?

As they put on their coats by the front door, Rodolfo faced Neftalí. "You heard Father. Put on your mittens."

Neftalí hesitated. His hands felt trapped inside mittens. They prevented him from picking up small treasures. He glanced up. Father could see them from where he still sat at the table. Reluctantly, Neftalí held out his hands while Rodolfo shoved the wool over his fingers.

Then Neftalí reached for his favorite hat, an old green oilskin that Father had given him. When he wore it, he imagined absorbing all of Father's authority through the brim.

"Are you really going to wear that ridiculous hat?" said Rodolfo. "Everyone will think you are a dunce."

Neftalí stood straighter and pulled the hat on tighter.

Annoyed, Rodolfo threw up his arms. "It is no wonder you have no friends." He took Neftalí's hand and led him out the door.

Like a determined toad, Rodolfo navigated the muddy street by leaping from stone to stone, pulling Neftalí along behind him.

Neftalí slid his hand from his brother's firm grip.

"Keep up with me!" called Rodolfo.

But Neftalí had already stopped to examine a clump of knotted roots protruding from the base of a beech tree.

Rodolfo went back, took his hand, and tugged him toward the school yard.

Neftalí tried to keep up, but then he saw the lonely boot that Laurita had described yesterday from the window. He jerked his hand from Rodolfo's and ran to retrieve it.

Rodolfo caught up to him, grabbed his arm, and pulled him up. "You are dim-witted. Why must we stop at every brainless thing? Can you not walk like other boys?" Rodolfo pushed him along, until Neftalí dug his heels into the ground and pointed at the sky.

"What now?" demanded Rodolfo.

A strong gust of wind had snatched away an umbrella. It rocked and swayed in flight. Neftalí stood hypnotized.

"It is an umbrella. Nothing more. Let us go!" Rodolfo shoved him into the yard of the boys' school.

Then, *el viento* grabbed the oilskin hat, lifted it from Neftalí's head, and tossed it back and forth. Neftalí pulled away from Rodolfo and ran to capture it. But each time he lunged forward, the wind swept it up again, as if playing keep-away.

Neftalí thought he heard the wind roar, until he realized it was Rodolfo and a group of boys laughing and pointing at his feeble attempts. Helpless, he watched the wind steal his hat until the green oilskin vanished into the highest reaches of the Araucanian woods.

When Neftalí finally turned toward the ridicule, he tried to puff up his chest and walk taller. But without Father's hat, the feeling of authority was gone.

A teacher stood on the steps of the old mansion converted to a schoolhouse and rang the bell. The boys ran toward their classes. Neftalí hurried forward, but then he noticed a beetle on a spotted leaf. He pulled off the mittens, tossed them aside, and bent down to inspect it.

He heard a sigh above him.

"Come on, Neftalí. It will not be good for either of us if you are late."

Neftalí looked up into Rodolfo's imploring face. He took his hand.

"Where are your mittens?"

Neftalí turned to where he had left them. But they were gone.

"No matter," said Rodolfo. "Hurry. They are closing the door."

"B-b-but Father will . . ."

"Good riddance." Rodolfo spat on the

ground. "Now he cannot force you to wear them. Come!"

Neftalí ran inside on the heels of Rodolfo. But before he went to his classroom, he peeked out a hallway window and saw that the wind had also possessed his mittens. They looked like ghostly hands waving good-bye in the Chilean sky.

Where were they headed? Whose hands would they cover next?

As Neftalí watched the mittens fly away, he felt as if a small piece of himself had taken flight, too. Would that part of him ever have a friend? Or amount to anything?

He waved and whispered, "*Adiós.*"

What does the wind give?

What does the wind take away?

Where is the storehouse of lost and found?

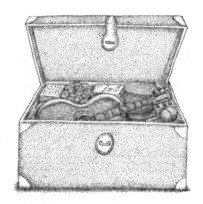

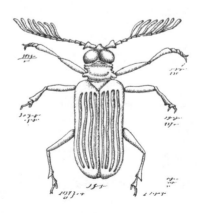

MUD

plip – plip

plop

oip, oip, oip, oip

tin,

tin,

tin,

tin,

tin

FOR A MONTH, THE CLOUDS SPILLED. Mountains slid into valleys, houses wallowed in shallow lakes, and the rocks and dirt that held fast to the train tracks disappeared. Father prepared to leave for work to repair the railroad and would be gone for several weeks.

From a window, Neftalí and Rodolfo watched him walk from the house to the platform to wait for the train. As the workers arrived, they huddled around him.

"Father does not have a sour face t-t-today," said Neftalí. "He looks happy and nice."

"He *is* happy," said Rodolfo. "He is the boss and everyone must follow his orders."

"But they l-l-like him," said Neftalí. "See how he jokes and the men laugh?"

Rodolfo shook his head. "You would laugh at his jokes, too, if you needed your job."

"Father has m-m-many friends," insisted Neftalí. "When he is home, our table is *always* crowded."

"Ah, yes. The great José Reyes. The more people at his table, the more important he feels. But he passes out invitations like overripe plums." Rodolfo's face twisted with disgust. "Better for us if he stays in the forest."

"Wh-why?"

"Neftalí, are you not miserable?" Rodolfo

held up one hand and began tapping each finger in sequence. "We cannot sit in the salon. We cannot eat unless our hands have been scrubbed raw. We cannot make noise. We cannot sing. We must think as he thinks." Rodolfo's shoulders sagged. "We can only *be* what he wants. Even Mamadre is a servant in his presence. We are all at his mercy. And as you get older, it gets worse."

"N-no, it will not get worse because I will not be stubborn like you."

"You think it is my fault? And that if you are obedient, you will grow up and be his pride and joy?" Rodolfo smirked. *"Buena suerte.* Good luck to that. When you are my age, you will see."

Outside, the whistle blew and the train pulled away. The boys watched until the caboose disappeared into the leafy cavern. "I wish *I* could go into the forest," said Neftalí.

"It is a long ride and not that much fun," said Rodolfo. "Why are you so eager?"

"I want to see . . . *everything*," said Neftalí. "The t-t-tall pines and parrots and beetles and eagles. And Father says there is a bird in the forest that tells the future."

Rodolfo nodded. "The chucao bird. If you hear it call on your right side, it is a good omen and means fortune and happiness. If you hear it call on your left, it is a warning and means bad luck and disappointment. They say the chucao bird does not lie. You will hear it before you ever see it, though. It is a very shy bird."

"*I* want to *see* the chucao bird. And I want to see the other Father . . . the n-n-nice one."

Rodolfo shook his head, then walked from the room.

Neftalí whispered, "I want to see . . . everything."

~ ~ ~

The days became weeks. The relentless rain forced everyone to stay indoors, and the mud prevented any wagon from maneuvering the streets.

Eventually, Uncle Orlando could not get to his office, so he came to Neftalí's house to write his newspaper articles at the kitchen table.

Uncle Orlando was Mamadre's younger brother and a taller version of her with the same wide face and brown, puppylike eyes. Neftalí loved to watch him work. He set up his own workplace at the table next to his uncle, imitating everything he did.

While Uncle Orlando wrote, Neftalí copied words from books. If Uncle Orlando looked up a word in the dictionary, Neftalí did the same. When Uncle Orlando tucked his pencil behind his ear, rose from the table, and paced back and forth, Neftalí shadowed him. The rain did not surrender, and neither did Neftalí.

On the fourth afternoon of Uncle Orlando's stay, Laurita played with her dolls on the kitchen floor, Rodolfo hummed as he did his homework, and Mamadre made potato turnovers for dinner. At one end of the table amid his papers and books, Uncle Orlando wrote. Neftalí stood next to him, leaning closer and closer.

"Nephew, I am not sure there is room for both of us in this chair unless you sit in my lap. Are you going to watch me write every single sentence?" asked Uncle Orlando.

Neftalí put his finger on Uncle Orlando's

paper. "What is that word?"

"That word is *Mapuche*. They are the indigenous people who live in Araucania – our neighbors."

Neftalí scooted his own piece of paper closer and copied the word.

"I suppose that if this keeps up, I will have to make you my partner someday."

Neftalí smiled and nodded vigorously.

"Well then, if you are going to assist me in my work, I will need to adjust the sound of your annoying breathing!" Uncle Orlando reached over and pulled Neftalí into his lap, tickling and wrestling with him. Soon they were rolling on the floor.

Rodolfo jumped up and pounced on them.

Laurita squealed as they moved dangerously close to her dolls.

The boys tumbled apart, laughing.

Mamadre stood with her hands on her hips. "I see that the dreariness of the rain has made us all need a diversion," she said. "Enough of sitting in this one room. Come. I will read to you in the salon."

"B-b-but we are n-n-not allowed in the salon," Neftalí reminded her.

Mamadre smiled and raised her eyebrows. "*Today* you are allowed."

While Mamadre and Uncle Orlando made

hot chocolate, Neftalí and Laurita and even Rodolfo giggled as they dragged blankets from their rooms to the salon.

Soon, they were all snuggled beneath the blankets and sipping the warm drinks. Mamadre picked up a book, cleared her throat, and began a story, transporting them to a land of elves and princesses.

When the story ended, Laurita flung off her coverlet, jumped up, and skipped in a circle. "I am a princess! I am a princess!"

Rodolfo teased. "You do not look like a princess."

Uncle Orlando looked at Mamadre. "No,

she does not. Can we do something about that?"

Mamadre smiled, rose from her chair, and kneeled at the giant brass-fitted trunk strapped with oak.

None of them had ever seen the contents of the trunk. Neftalí looked at Rodolfo, who smiled and shrugged. Laurita pressed her hands over her mouth in anticipation.

Mamadre lifted the heavy curved lid.

The smell of musty clothes and cedar drew Neftalí closer.

Mamadre took out a stack of folded dresses, a wool coat, and a fur hat, which she handed to Neftalí. Farther down, Mamadre found a lace petticoat and a filmy scarf. Laurita quickly pulled the petticoat over her clothes. As she twirled around, Mamadre lifted out a guitar. Uncle Orlando retrieved it and began to tighten and tune the strings.

Mamadre found a top hat, which she presented to Rodolfo.

While Mamadre tied Laurita's scarf, Neftalí stepped to the trunk. He peered over the edge. At the bottom, he saw a bundle of letters and postcards, tied with a satin ribbon. How many words had been saved inside?

He leaned forward, reached down, grabbed the bundle . . . and fell in headfirst!

Mamadre spun around. "Neftalí!"

His muffled voice came from the bottom of the trunk. "I am here."

When Uncle Orlando lifted him up and set him on the sofa, Neftalí still held the bundle. Each letter had been opened from the top of the envelope, the flaps still sealed with wax and stamped with the impression of a heart. On the top letter, someone had written the word *love* above the seal.

Mamadre took the bundle from him, put it back inside, and carefully closed the trunk. "Neftalí, the lid could have fallen on your head. Or your hands. And for what? Some old letters and cards from relatives we do not even know? Promise me you will never open this trunk!"

Neftalí looked wistfully toward it. "I p-p-promise."

Uncle Orlando strummed the guitar. "Neftalí, come stand next to me. As my partner, how do you think we should proceed?"

Neftalí looked up. "With a s-s-song?"

"My sentiments exactly," he said, propping one foot on a chair and the guitar on his knee. "Rodolfo? Will you honor us? No one in the family can sing as you can." He began to play.

Rodolfo hesitated and looked from Mama-dre to Uncle Orlando for reassurance.

"Your father is not here, Rodolfo. And it would be a favor to me."

Rodolfo turned back to Mamadre.

She nodded.

Something deep inside of Neftalí wanted Rodolfo to sing at the top of his lungs. He clapped wildly. "Y-y-yes!" he said.

Rodolfo smiled and put on the top hat. He began, softly at first. *"Libiamo, libiamo ne'lieti calici che la belleza infiora. . . ."* Let us drink from the goblets of joy adorned with beauty. . . .

He stopped and looked to each of them for reassurance.

Uncle Orlando nodded. "Continue. I know

the song. From *La Traviata*. But sing louder and faster. It is a song of great spirit." He strummed the opening chords.

Rodolfo began again.

Mamadre and Laurita danced.

Neftalí stood up, tapped his foot, and clapped to the beat.

Laurita and Mamadre waltzed faster and faster, both of them laughing.

Neftalí could not take his eyes from Rodolfo's face, which had lost all traces of anger and sullenness. His voice was deep and rich and operatic.

Rodolfo opened his arms wide and sang,

his tenor round and full and so beautiful that Neftalí's eyes filled with tears.

Uncle Orlando finished the song with several resounding chords to accompany Rodolfo's last long note.

Rodolfo took off the hat and swept it in a great arc. As he bowed, Mamadre and Laurita rushed to hug him.

"*¡B-b-bravo!*" yelled Neftalí.

Neftalí could not remember if he had ever seen Rodolfo or Laurita so happy. Or the last time he had heard Mamadre laugh out loud. He ran to his family and threw his arms around them, wanting this elation to last forever.

But all too soon, Mamadre's body grew rigid. She raised a hand and tilted her head to one side.

No one spoke as they listened for what Mamadre had heard. There it was. A faint train whistle. Although any number of trains passed through Temuco every day, she always knew the sound of Father's. Her smile faded.

Neftalí watched Rodolfo's face drain.

"Do not worry," said Mamadre. "The train is not yet near. Now, quickly . . ."

They all scrambled.

Rodolfo and Uncle Orlando replaced the contents of the trunk. Laurita hurried to collect the cups and saucers. But her hand trembled so much that a cup fell to the floor and shattered. She began to cry.

Neftalí rushed to her. "It is all right, Laurita. You p-p-pull the blankets back to the bedrooms. I will pick up the pieces."

Wide-eyed, Laurita sniffled. "But – but . . ."

"If Father notices, I will say that *I* dropped it," said Neftalí.

She swiped an arm across her tears, gave him a sweet smile, and began gathering the blankets.

Meanwhile, Mamadre glided from one preparation to another: from the kitchen for a tablecloth to the dining room, from the cabinet for candelabras to the table. Attentive and method-ical, she folded napkins and set out glasses and plates without saying a word.

After Neftalí cleaned up the cups and saucers, he rushed to help Rodolfo and Uncle Orlando carry extra chairs to the table. He already dreaded all of the adults who might look him in the eye and ask him questions.

"How m-m-m-many chairs?"

Mamadre answered without looking up. "Twelve, at least. If Father does not bring home that many guests, he will fill every place with strangers from the street. Comb your hair. Wash your hands. I must go and warm *las empanadas y el bistec.*"

Neftali's mouth watered at the suggestion of the potato turnovers and the steak smothered with onions. He hoped they would fill up the empty feeling that had overcome him at the sound of the train whistle – the feeling that he had suddenly lost something.

He watched Mamadre turn and walk to the kitchen, her face now wan and preoccupied. What had happened to her laughter and twinkling eyes and flushed cheeks? Where had Mamadre buried them?

~ ~ ~

Within the hour, Father's boots pounded on the floorboards. His big voice filled the house. *"¡Aquí estoy!"* I am here! He blew the conductor's whistle.

Neftalí, Rodolfo, and Laurita rushed to stand in front of him. They held their hands flat and then turned their palms up for inspection. Neftalí's were still pink from his vigorous scrubbing.

"Satisfactory." Father nodded and then headed toward the dining room.

The door opened again, and men began to flood into the house: railroad workers, shopkeepers, even a traveling merchant who had been waylaid overnight in Temuco.

Father poured drinks from the sideboard and assigned everyone a seat.

Neftalí sat in his chair with his best posture and studied his plate, avoiding any of the guests' eyes. He pushed the tablecloth aside and looked longingly underneath. If only he could escape to the shadowy company of boots.

Father sat at the head of the table, jovial and generous to his guests, passing around stories as easily as he passed around *el pan amasado*, the homemade bread. He told tales about Percheron horses, pumas in the wild, and the Mapuche Indians.

"What is the current situation with the

Mapuche?" asked the merchant.

"We are trying to move them out of the area," said a shopkeeper. "But many will not listen. These are difficult times for those of us who are trying to develop the land and make a nice community here in Temuco."

Uncle Orlando cleared his throat. "The Mapuche people have lived here for hundreds of years. Why should they leave their homeland?" He had a fire in his belly and a determination in his eyes.

Neftalí admired how his uncle never had a problem speaking out about what he thought was right or wrong. Would *Neftalí* ever have the confidence to do the same?

"Their presence is undesirable," said the shopkeeper. "They do not want to conform to the ways of the townspeople. The Mapuche cannot even read. The shopkeepers must put up a sign shaped like a giant shoe above the shoe store, and a sign shaped like a giant hammer above the hardware store . . . a giant key for the locksmith. It is absurd. And all this so they will know which building is which?"

That was true, thought Neftalí. He had seen those very signs. The giant shoe was his favorite.

"And what is wrong with that?" asked Uncle

Orlando. "Why do we not learn a little of their language? *We* came to *their* land. Why should they think as we think? Why should they give up everything they have known for generations?"

Neftalí considered Uncle Orlando's words. He could not imagine being pushed from his own home without his books and his collections. Not to mention leaving his school and the river Cautín. His eyes followed the conversation from one man to the other. Their voices grew sharper with each response.

"It is progress," said the shopkeeper. "For me, it is business, nothing more, nothing less."

"Nothing less than greed," said Uncle

Orlando. "Your thinking is as thick as the mud!"

"Wait a moment," said the shopkeeper, studying Uncle Orlando. "I know who you are. You are the one who owns *La Mañana,* the newspaper that publishes all the articles *in favor* of the Mapuche."

Uncle Orlando stood up.

Neftalí's eyes grew wide with fear. The shopkeeper was much larger than Uncle Orlando.

"Gentlemen! This is a family dinner!" said Father. "We will discuss the Mapuche at a more appropriate time."

Uncle Orlando sat down and folded his

arms across his chest.

The shopkeeper speared his meat with his fork and ate it. He chewed vigorously, his eyes darting from one person to the next.

No one said a word.

Mamadre rose from the table. Her chair scraped the floor, breaking the uncomfortable silence.

Father pointed at one of his workers. "Tell the children about the beetle you found yesterday."

Neftalí sat up a little straighter and strained to hear.

"I found it on a *luma* tree. It looked like a

living jewel wearing many fantastic colors – pink, green, purple, and silver. And when I tried to catch the thing, it zipped away. One moment it was there and the next . . . *poof!*" He nodded at Neftalí. "Young man, have you ever been into the forest?"

All eyes turned to Neftalí. He knew he must answer when an adult spoke to him. But his skin felt as if it were tightening and blood rushed to his cheeks.

"N-n-n-n-n-n . . . " The word could not escape. He tried again. "N-n-n-n-n –"

Father shifted in his chair. His face reddened. "Do not pay attention to him. He is absentminded. And he spends so much time in idle thought he can barely speak. There's no telling what will become of him."

Neftalí sat with his eyes cast down, paralyzed. Was he breathing? He could not tell.

"There is nothing wrong with a little idle thought," said Uncle Orlando. "And perhaps he needs the athletic outdoors and a trip to the great forest where he can focus on what is real – this beautiful land and its people – before a developer tries to change it." He glanced at Neftalí. "Nephew, you would like that, would you not?"

Neftalí lifted his eyes slightly and nodded.

Father grunted. "Maybe next year, when

he is not so feeble." He turned to Mamadre. "Let us take coffee. Children, you are excused."

Grateful to be released, Neftalí slid from his chair and ran to his room. There, with the muffled voices of the grown-ups in the background, he paused before his collections. He straightened the rows of rocks, twigs, and nests, touching each item as if taking attendance. Father's word echoed.

Absentminded. Absentminded.

It did not make sense. How could he be absentminded when his head was so crowded with thoughts?

He opened the drawer and unfolded each piece of paper he had saved. Then he read the words, mouthing each one perfectly. Before he replaced them, he added one more: *luma*.

Later, as he lay in bed, Neftalí tried to imagine the beetle on the *luma* tree, the one that looked like a living jewel and could disappear in the blink of an eye.

Father's words haunted him.

Neftalí wished that time would disappear as fast as the colorful beetle – in one *poof* – so he, too, could discover what would become of him.

What is the color of a minute?

A month?

A year?

I am poetry,

lurking in dappled shadow.

I am the confusion

of root

and gnarled branch.

I am the symmetry

of insect,

leaf,

and a bird's outstretched wings.

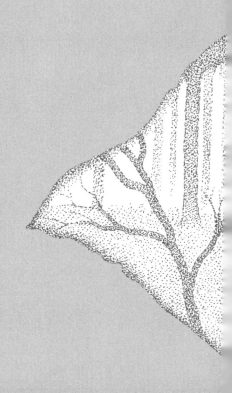

FOREST

"THOSE ARE WEEDS, NEFTALÍ," said Rodolfo. "Not flowers. Now, come. If you make me late for school again, I will tell Father. And today I do not feel like running."

Neftalí stopped picking the tiny blossoms that made the spring air smell peppery. He stuffed the ones he'd collected into his pocket and hurried toward Rodolfo.

Surprised, Rodolfo put his hands on his hips and stared at him. "So today you are listening to me?"

"I do not want to get into any t-trouble. Only three more days until Father takes me on the train to the forest. I am old enough now. I am eight. And strong enough, too." He held up an arm and tried to make a muscle.

Rodolfo pulled his coat tighter around him. "Good for you. I don't care if I *ever* go back."

"That is because you g-get to go with Father all the time. What did you see last week?"

Rodolfo didn't answer. He just took Neftalí's hand, looked straight ahead, and pulled him toward school.

"Birds? D-did you see birds?" Neftalí persisted.

Rodolfo sighed. "Yes. I saw birds. I even saw the timid chucao. And Mr. Chucao Bird gave me a warning."

Neftalí tugged on Rodolfo's hand, stopping him. "How did you know it was the chucao bird?"

"Easy. Its call sounds just like its name. *Chew-cow.* It is a tiny bird with a throat the color of copper. But its size is deceiving. It has a very loud voice."

"Did you hear it on your right side or on your left?"

"On my left," said Rodolfo.

"Did you have bad luck?"

Rodolfo scuffed the ground with his boot. "A bit."

"But if you heard the call on your left, why didn't you just turn around" – Neftalí quickly faced the other direction – "so that the bird was on your right? Then you would have *good* luck."

Rodolfo rolled his eyes. "There is only one antidote to the warning. And that is to take off a piece of clothing – a hat, a shoe, your shirt – and immediately put it back on. If you do it in time, you erase the bad luck. I took off my hat."

"Did you take it off quickly enough?

Did it erase your bad luck?"

Rodolfo frowned. "Most of it . . ." It was as if a dark cloud had descended upon Rodolfo. He took Neftalí's hand and tugged him toward school again.

"What happened? Did you get stung by a hornet?"

"It is not important."

"What else did you see in the forest, then?" asked Neftalí.

Rodolfo ignored him.

"You must have seen *something*. . . . Eagles? D-did you see eagles? And what about Father? What was he like? Tell me. *Porfa* . . . "

"Stop your begging!" Rodolfo snapped. "And don't ask me again. Or I'll tell Father you *did* make me late for school. And then you can forget about your precious trip to the forest."

What was wrong with Rodolfo? Was he jealous that it was Neftalí's turn? Or was he just ungrateful?

When they reached the school yard, Rodolfo released his hand. "Go to your classroom. And if you're thinking you're going to find your so-called *nice* Father in the forest, you might be disappointed. So do not hope for too much." He turned and walked away with his head down and his hands in his pockets.

As Neftalí watched him go, he noticed that Rodolfo was limping.

~ ~ ~

Three days later, Neftalí opened his eyes in the faint light before sunrise. It was much too early to get up. He stared at the ceiling, imagining all of the things he might collect and bring home from the forest.

Then, the cracks in the ceiling opened and let in the sky. He found himself lying in his bed beneath an enormous tree with a wide trunk. He got up, put on his boots, and marched around the tree, counting his steps to determine how many it would take to make the complete circle.

"Forty-three, forty-four, forty-five . . ." His bed marked where he had begun, but no matter how many steps he took, he could not get around the girth of the trunk to reach it again. Finally, Neftalí decided to climb the gargantuan tree, hoping to find a way *over* it, instead of around it. He was high in the branches when he heard Father's voice.

"Neftalí, did you wear your boots all night long?"

Neftalí dropped from the tree to the bed.

Father hovered over him, wearing a dark gray cape, one Neftalí had never seen before.

Neftalí sat up and stared at the boots on

his feet. "I w-wanted to be ready." He jumped to the floor, his heart beating with anticipation.

"Slow down," said Father, laughing quietly. "You have plenty of time. Get dressed and eat breakfast. And wear something warm. The morning air will chill you."

Neftalí pointed at Father. "The c-cape?"

"Ah, yes. It is new. The company gave it to me, for my service. The finest wool. When you are ready, meet me on the platform." He turned and marched from the room, the cape billowing behind him.

~ ~ ~

When Neftalí arrived in the kitchen,

Rodolfo was already sitting at the table, eating *una marraqueta*.

Mamadre nodded to a place for Neftalí, where another bread roll waited to be slathered with jam.

Sleepy-eyed, Laurita wandered into the kitchen, dragging a rag doll. Mamadre picked her up, hugged her, and set her on a chair. Then she handed Neftalí a bag. "Bread, fruit, and cheese for later. It will be a long day on the train and you will be hungry."

"I wish I could go on the train," said Laurita.

"You are too little," said Neftalí. "You

must be big like me. Right, Rodolfo?"

Rodolfo said nothing and looked only at his food.

It wasn't until Laurita dribbled jam on her lap and Mamadre ushered her from the kitchen to change her clothes that Rodolfo put down his fork and leaned forward. "Neftalí, look at me and listen carefully. When you go with Father, you must follow his orders. Do not get underfoot of the workers. I did once and he made me sit in the train all morning. And do not talk to the workers unless they talk to you first. Otherwise Father will think you are keeping them from their work. Another thing . . . and this is very important."

Rodolfo leaned across the table and put his hand on Neftalí's arm. "Are you listening?"

Neftalí nodded.

"When he blows the whistle, get back to the train immediately so that he does not have to come looking for you. That is where I made my mistake. Last week . . . when it was time to go, he had to search for me. When he found me, I was disobeying him. He . . . he . . ." Rodolfo winced. "I . . . I still have the bruises. Do you understand? You do *not* want Father to catch you doing something . . . wrong."

Neftalí's heart sank into his stomach. "What were you d-d-doing?"

For a few moments, Rodolfo gazed off. Then he let go of Neftalí's arm, pushed himself away from the table, and stood up. He took a few shaky steps toward the door, turned, and said, "I was singing."

Which is sharper?

The hatchet that cuts down dreams?

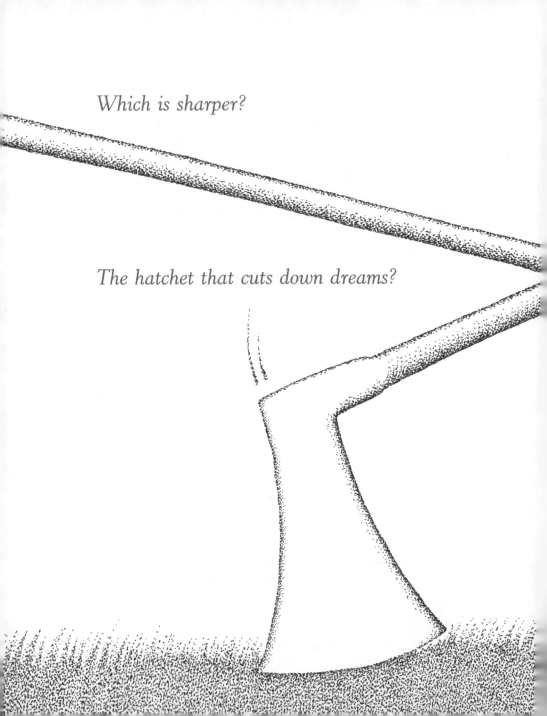

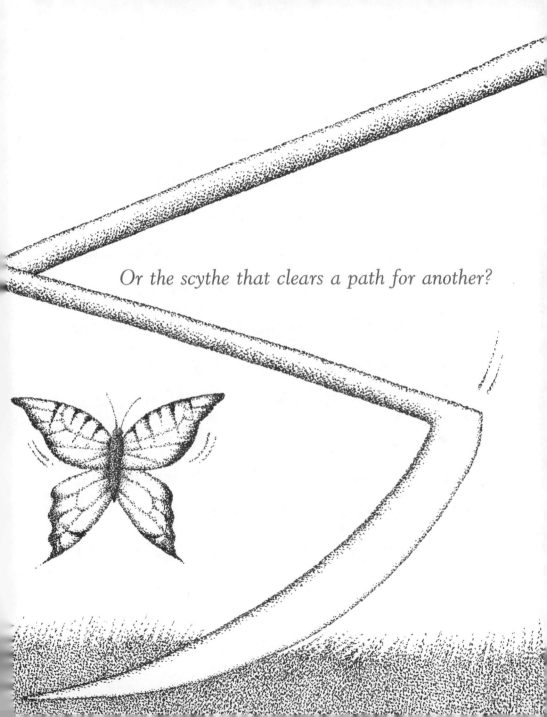

Or the scythe that clears a path for another?

Under a veil of steam, Neftalí traveled on the chuffing train deep into the rain forest. As he looked out the window, he thought carefully about Rodolfo's advice. On the outside, he had followed all of Father's instructions: He had worn a wool sweater, he had sat up front in the seat next to Father, he had not fidgeted or climbed on the bench, he had not spoken to any of the workers nor drawn attention to himself. On the inside, he jumped up and down with excitement. His stomach quivered, and he secretly kept pinching himself to make sure he was not dreaming.

After several hours, the engine stopped. The sturdy men clambered from the train. Neftalí followed Father, stepping down into a world of conifers.

His senses whirled and he felt giddy. He could not turn his head fast enough to absorb it all: tiny needles of light piercing the canopy, the untamed overgrowth of plants and trees, the musty smell of giant mushrooms, the crisp fragrance of pine, the sudden shrieks and flight of parrots.

Father stood next to him, blowing his whistle and giving orders to the men, who set to work quarrying stone rubble.

"See?" said Father. "The men shovel the rocks onto the hods, those cradles set crosswise on the poles. Then, two men, one on each end, lift them and dump the rock onto the train cars. Another day, it will be hauled to a stretch of track and will become the ballast to anchor the washed-out rails."

Fascinated, Neftalí nodded and watched the men lift the hods and march to the train, their bodies already glistening with perspiration.

"Stay nearby. I will signal when it is time for lunch." Father hurried toward the workers.

Neftalí was grateful to explore alone. Reverently, he crept into the forest, but not too far. Even just a short distance from the train, it was as if he were in a great domed cathedral – in a world without sky.

He stopped every few steps, examining the novelties: the bellies of gigantic fronds, the luminescent wings of insects, bird feathers, and pods that had dropped from the canopy. He collected pockets full of twigs and slippery partridge eggs. He overturned dead limbs to find the hollows where spiders lived.

All morning, Neftalí wandered, inhaling the scent of wet leaves, wild herbs, and cinnamon. With a stick, he cleared a swath of damp earth and wrote on it. Slowly, he murmured the words to the trees, delighting in the tempos they played on his tongue.

CHUCAO

RAULI

LIANA

LUMA

HIERBA

COPIHUE

MASUCHE

PUMA

Neftalí looked around to see if anyone was near. If Father had heard or seen him, would he have thought him absentminded? Was he doing something wrong?

He smudged out the words and kicked the leaves back in place.

He heard a rustling inside a rotting log and bent to peek inside. A gigantic horned beetle scurried from beneath the leaves. At first Neftalí jerked back, but then he bent closer to watch it hiss. He had never seen a beetle so big or fierce-looking.

"He is a monster, no?"

Neftalí jumped at the voice. He looked up to see Father looming over him. Had he blown his whistle and Neftalí had not heard? But Father did not *look* angry.

"It is a rhinoceros beetle," said Father. "He is so strong that he can carry a log eight hundred times heavier than his own weight. See his horns? He uses them to fight. He is a king." He patted Neftalí on the back. "It will be time for lunch soon. Come back to the train in a few minutes."

Neftalí nodded and watched him walk away, swaggering beneath the dark cape, with the confidence of someone who owned the forest.

Neftalí turned back to the beetle. How could something so small overcome and carry a burden so large? What magic did it possess?

As he marveled at the beetle, the shell contorted and bulged, growing bigger and bigger. Its legs elongated until it was as tall as a pony.

Neftalí looked on with fascination.

Two giant beady eyes looked back.

The rhinoceros beetle moved closer. When it was inches from Neftalí, it folded its front legs, and lowered its hideous head, as if it were deferring to him. Then it made a tiny squeak.

Oddly unafraid, Neftalí climbed onto its sturdy back, and rode it through the forest, harnessing all of its strange strength.

What lies beneath the bravado

of a black and shiny armor?

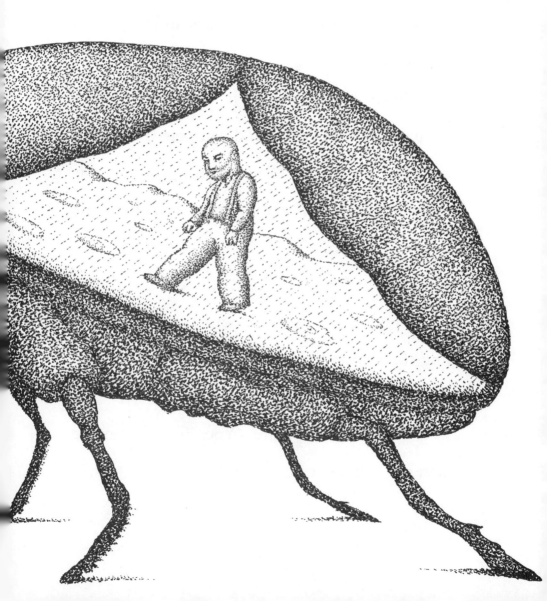

At lunch, Neftalí sat next to Father. He listened to the workers banter back and forth with good-natured teasing.

Even Father joined in, until he paused, pointed to a nearby tree, and whispered, "Shush."

Neftalí turned to see another beetle, this one a shimmering rainbow. He sucked in his breath. The living jewel!

In wonder, they all sat still and quiet.

Suddenly, a parrot swooped overhead, startling the insect. In an instant, the beetle became a flash of color, then disappeared.

Father nudged him. "Your first day in the forest and you see such a thing! You have the luck."

One of the men tossed Neftalí a tomato. "So, how do you like this life on the ballast train?"

Before Neftalí could answer, Father draped an arm around his shoulder. "He likes it fine," he said. "After all, he is a railroader's son."

Neftalí looked at the ground, grinning from ear to ear. So *this* was the other Father.

"Will he be a conductor, too?" asked another.

"Most definitely *not*," said Father. "He has bigger plans. He will be a doctor or a dentist."

Neftalí looked up at Father. A doctor or dentist? How did Father know what Neftalí would become when he did not know himself?

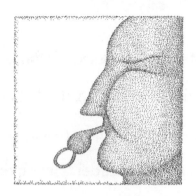

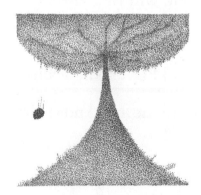

TREE

ALL AFTERNOON, NEFTALÍ EXPLORED the great
forest, drifting farther away from the train until
he came upon a towering pine in a small clearing.
He looked up at its height and wondered what
it had seen from its branches. Did it hide all the
secrets of the forest within its dark nooks? Did it
know, too, what Neftalí would become?

He scoured the ground around the tree and

found a scattering of pinecones closed as tight as fists. He searched and found one that had opened, large and bulbous, and was dotted with pearls of sap. He carefully spun it on his palm. The scales resembled a carousel of iridescent wings. He turned it upside down. It looked like a cascade of miniature umbrellas. Lifting it with both hands, he considered its beauty.

Then, in gratitude, Neftalí gazed up at the great tree that had bestowed such a treasure. "Thank you," he whispered.

Something moved in its branches.

Neftalí carefully scanned each limb. There was nothing but the gentle movement of pine needles from a soft breeze. He kept his post and soon saw the movement again.

An eagle sat on a limb high above his head, looking down on him.

Neftalí was afraid to move, afraid to startle it. He watched it turn its head as if appraising the forest, preen its chest, and shake out its feathers. Then, with the elegance of a dancer, it lifted its wings and, in a display of white underpinnings, leaped into the sky.

Neftalí watched until he could no longer see it. He looked around and sighed. He longed to tell someone about the eagle and the pinecone. He longed to share *all* that he had seen with a friend, someone whose hands he could squeeze with excitement, someone with whom he might be able to talk without stammering. He wished it with all of his heart.

He even dared to think that he could share it all with Father.

He would wait until they rode the train home together. Father's work would be done by then, and it would be just the two of them, side by side on the train. There would be hours for Neftalí to tell him about the eagle and show him the pinecone.

He smiled as he walked from the clearing back through the forest, until he heard the call.

chew-chew-chew-chew-cow

chew-chew-chew-chew-cow

chew-chew-cow

chew-cow

chew-chew-chew-chew-cow

The chucao bird! From which direction was it coming? If it called on his right side, it meant good luck and happiness. If it called on his left, it meant bad luck and disappointment. And it never lied.

Neftalí spun around. But now he was confused and could not tell where it was. Just in case, he quickly set down the pinecone, removed his sweater, and put it back on. He retrieved the pinecone and listened.

Chew-chew-chew-chew-cow.

He heard the call again. This time he was sure it was on his right! Good luck. Maybe even for what he had wished for today: a close friend and Father's affection. Neftalí grinned. As he turned, he saw the chucao bird flitting from a fallen log to a low branch to the duff on the forest floor. It sang again. Rodolfo was right. It was small but louder than anything he had heard in the forest, except for Father's whistle, which now sent out a shrieking signal.

Neftalí headed straight for the train, stopping only to pick up a furry caterpillar. Later, he would show it to Father and ask him to identify it.

When he arrived at the locomotive, Father and the workers stood together, talking. Slowly, Neftalí approached, balancing all of his treasures.

The men began to chuckle.

Neftalí looked down at himself. His front pockets bulged. Sticks sprouted from his back pockets, along with trailing vines. Small feathers and dried leaves that had stuck in his hair fell to the ground. The pinecone lay cradled in one hand, the squirming caterpillar in the other. Now the men laughed louder at the spectacle.

Neftalí saw Father's cheeks pink with embarrassment. He sucked in his breath, overwhelmed with the idea that he had drawn attention to himself. Had he been a fanatic? How would Father react to this shame?

Quickly, he set the pinecone and the

caterpillar on a nearby rock and removed the contents of his front pockets: bird eggs, waxy leaves, the tip of a fox's tail. He pulled the sticks and vines from his back pockets and tossed them aside. He reached up and tousled his hair. Dust and duff rained over him.

The men howled with laughter.

Father's face tightened and turned to stone. "Enough nonsense. Everyone to the train. It is time to go." He turned and marched away.

Neftalí couldn't bear to leave the pinecone behind. He snatched it up, tucked it under his sweater, and climbed aboard. In his seat, he huddled as close as possible to the window.

A worker paused beside him, as if to say something. But before the man could open his mouth, Father bellowed, "Ignore the boy! He is an idiot!"

The man gave Neftalí a sympathetic nod and moved down the aisle.

When the train started, Neftalí waited for Father to come and sit with him. But he never did. All the way to Temuco, Neftalí stared out the window, hugged the pinecone, and wondered if, for the first time, the chucao bird had lied.

~ ~ ~

At home, Neftalí studied the altar of his found treasures until he found a place of honor.

He straightened the orderly rows: feathers, eggs, leaves, stones, nests, pods, twigs, and now his pinecone, sitting sentry over all else. Each time Neftalí touched an object, he imagined the stories a creature might have told while crossing the token's path: a caterpillar to the veined leaf, a snake to the twig, a fox to the seedpod.

Tired from the long day, he climbed into bed and closed his eyes.

That night, the pinecone journeyed with him to a star, far, far away from Temuco.

What wisdom does the eagle whisper

to those who are learning to fly?

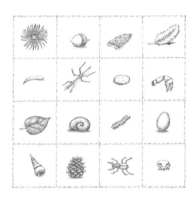

PINECONE

Neftalí heard Father's boots pounding up the steps. He lowered his book and waited, hoping that he would not be summoned. The boots tramped through the house and, as he suspected, the whistle blasted. Neftalí closed his eyes, wincing. Why couldn't he be left alone to read?

Since the visit to the forest a month ago, Neftalí had avoided Father and spent every free moment hidden away in his room consumed with the books of Jules Verne. Neftalí reluctantly put down *Journey to the Center of the Earth.* Instead of hurrying, though, he walked slowly and deliberately. He found Father pacing in the salon.

"You need to come *promptly*, Neftalí. What were you doing?"

"Reading, Father."

"You are nothing more than a brittle twig," he barked. "And this obsession with books will not make you vigorous! Have we not talked about this time and again? Do you want to be a scatterbrain for the rest of your life?"

"N-no, Father."

"You need to be outside instead of squandering good weather. Now run and play with the other boys. And none of your diversions. Join the games and let them make a man of you."

With Father watching, Neftalí headed outside. He put his hands in his pockets and meandered down the road toward the boys who were playing *fútbol*.

Ahead, Laurita's friend, Valeria, and her older sister, Blanca, walked toward him. Blanca often escorted Valeria to the house to play with Laurita. Although Neftalí had never admitted it to anyone, he secretly thought Blanca was kind and pretty. Seeing her now, even from a distance, made him blush.

As the two girls drew closer, Neftalí stared at the ground.

"Hello, Neftalí," said Blanca.

For the briefest moment, he looked up and then back down. His heart pounded. Blanca had smiled at him! He wanted to answer, but his throat felt so tight that he could barely swallow. He kept his chin pressed to his chest and continued walking. After a dozen steps, he glanced back to make sure they had disappeared down the road and then he blew out a deep breath. What was *wrong* with him that he couldn't say hello in return? Had Blanca thought him a fool? Would she ever speak to him again?

To calm himself, he inspected the remnants of a recent storm. He loitered over the oily colors of street puddles, rust-colored and green, like Blanca's hair and eyes. He inspected the frazzled strips of bark, dangling from a tree like Blanca's flowing skirt. He admired the newly arrived pebbles that had settled on the side of the road, their faces as smooth as a pool of cream, like Blanca's skin.

Neftalí?

Had someone whispered his name? He stood and turned around.

Nearby, Rodolfo kicked a ball back and

forth to Guillermo, the new boy from school. Guillermo was just a year older than Neftalí, but was the same size as the much older Rodolfo. The burly athlete had been at their school only a few weeks, and he'd already been in a number of fights. Neftalí hoped that, like so many, he and his family would stay a few months in Temuco and then move on.

Neftalí?

There it was again. Had Rodolfo called to him? Did he want Neftalí to join their game? He ran toward them.

Seeing him, Guillermo yelled, "Shinbone! Shinbone! Do not let him play!" He and Rodolfo looked only at the ball being passed between them, as if Neftalí were invisible.

So it had not been Rodolfo calling his name. Who was it then?

Neftalí searched from one end of the street to the other but saw no one looking his way. Maybe Father was right. Maybe he *was* a scatter-brain. He looked down and saw a long stick, just the right length for dragging, and picked it up. He turned back toward home. When he arrived in his backyard, he wrote on the earth:

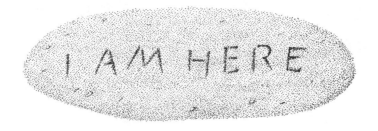

Neftalí studied the house and his bedroom window where he often stood to gaze at the hole in the fence. Then he turned and walked to the corner of the yard. Where was the opening? He cleared away the brambles until he found the spot, now jammed with leaves and mud. With the stick, he poked and scraped until the gap was clear. Then he crouched down and peered through to the other side.

Next door, the flowers bowed their heads toward one another. The trees reached out in leafy embraces. Even the thistles clumped together like old friends. As usual, though, the porthole revealed nothing more than another weed-choked yard.

A prickly sensation washed over him, and the hair stood up on his arms. He sensed a presence and thought he heard a small intake of breath. He pulled back. After a few moments, he peeked through again. Still nothing. Had he wished so hard for someone to be there that he had imagined a ghost?

Suddenly, the hand of a child darted through the hole and disappeared. Neftalí jerked away, his heart thumping. The hand reappeared and nudged a toy sheep through the gap. Neftalí picked it up. The wheels on which the sheep had once rolled were gone. The wool was matted and yellowed. But Neftalí did not care. There *was* someone on the other side. His thoughts toppled. Was it someone new to Temuco? Or someone from the street?

The desire to give something back overwhelmed Neftalí. But what could he offer? What could he pass through the hole in the fence that was as remarkable?

He raced into the house, to his room, and then back outside. Breathless, Neftalí laid his offering in the opening to the stranger's world. He heard a gasp of appreciation and watched the hands lift the pinecone away.

Neftalí looked through the hole, but could not see anyone. He heard only the thudding of retreating footsteps, a clumping of footfalls on wooden stairs, and a swollen door yelping shut. Was the child shy, too? Was he or she waiting for Neftalí to be the first to say hello?

Clutching the sheep, he hurried to the front yard and hid beneath a sprawling bush, watching the house next door. No one went in or came out. He stroked the sheep and waited. Still no one came.

Finally, he crossed into the neighboring yard. Taking one shaky step, then another, he climbed the uneven wooden steps. His mouth felt dry. Would he be able to speak without stuttering? His hands perspired and his clothes felt as if they were much too small. He hesitated. What if this child was like Guillermo? Neftalí reassured himself that someone so generous could not be cruel. He stretched out his hand and knocked. At his touch, the door creaked open.

He took a few steps inside.

The bare floors were interrupted only by discarded boxes, spiderwebs, and the occasional animal dropping. As Neftalí wandered through a house long deserted, his footsteps echoed on the wooden floors, the sound hollow and empty.

The giver could have been anyone in the world.

What grows in the dark soil

of disappointment?

As the seasons changed, the sheep became Neftalí's devoted companion. In the fall, he buried his head in its wool to protect himself from the boys at school, who chased him and pelted him with acorns.

During the winter rains, Neftalí read out loud to the sheep, and together they traveled to distant worlds.

In the spring, when he should have been studying his mathematics, it sat with him in a wild apple tree on the banks of the river Cautín, daydreaming.

And when summer bloomed yellow-hot and the family prepared for a trip to the sea, the sheep sat on top of Neftalí's belongings, waiting to be packed.

For weeks, all Father had talked about was "his great summer plan." Neftalí was excited, too, but something about Father's overzealous enthusiasm pried a tiny splinter of doubt from his mind.

Neftalí reached for his sheep and pulled it close. He whispered, "Do not worry, *amigo*. I will protect you."

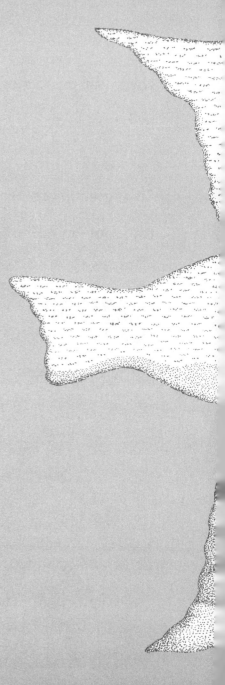

I am poetry,

prowling the blue,

tempting my prey

with fish, shell, and sky.

From beneath the eyelids

of the deep, I seek

the unsuspecting heart.

Look.

Look at me.

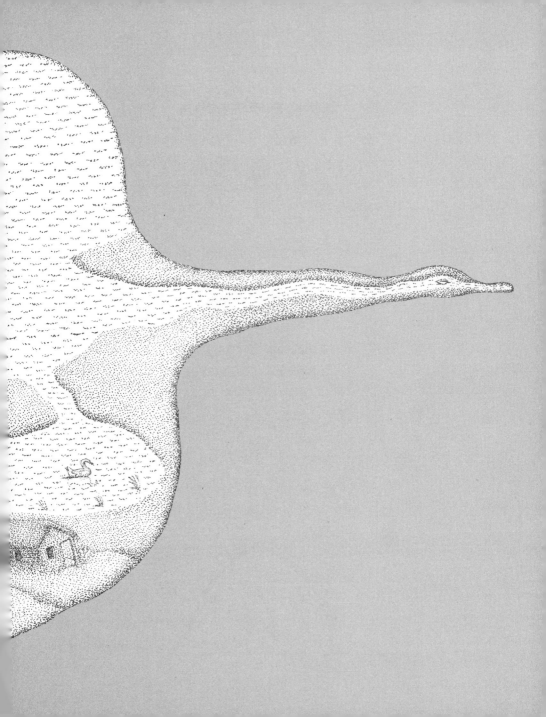

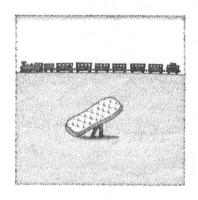

RIVER

NEFTALÍ AND LAURITA WATCHED from the window as Father carried several boxes to the train platform. Uncle Orlando and Rodolfo followed, carrying a mattress.

"Why m-must we take dishes and beds?" Neftalí asked Mamadre, who was folding blankets and arranging them on the floor.

"Because the summerhouse that Father's

friend has offered us has no furnishings. So we will take some of our household with us."

"Why must we leave in the middle of the night?" asked Laurita.

"We need to meet the riverboat before dawn, and it is a very long way," said Mamadre. "First, we will take the train to Carahue. Then load all of our things onto an oxcart that will take us to the dock. There we will get on a boat with a big wheel and travel down the Imperial River toward the ocean, until we reach Puerto Saavedra."

"But my collections . . . and my books."

"No one will touch them, Neftalí. All of your things will be here waiting when we return.

And you may bring a *few* books in case there is a rainy day. But Father wants you to spend your time outdoors."

Neftalí nodded. "To b-become robust, like Rodolfo. I wish he could come, too. Can't the hardware store let him have a holiday?"

Mamadre shook her head. "He has not worked there long enough. And Father went to great effort to arrange this job for him."

"But he has never *been* to the ocean."

"Yes, he has been," said Mamadre. "You just do not remember. When you and Laurita were much too young to travel, Father took him one summer."

"If Rodolfo cannot come, there is r-room for Uncle Orlando, then," Neftalí tried.

"Uncle Orlando is very busy at *La Mañana* right now. The newspaper is sponsoring a fair to sell Mapuche arts and crafts in a few weeks. I already gave him money to buy a blanket. Do not worry. You and Laurita will have each other. And . . . I am hoping the holiday will be a good rest for Father."

"Where will we sleep tonight if our mattresses are on the train?" Laurita watched Rodolfo carrying another one to the platform.

Mamadre motioned toward the blankets on the floor. "I have made a little bed for you both.

When it is time to leave, I will come for you."

After Mamadre settled them on the blankets and left, Laurita whispered, "Neftalí, I'm scared."

"Of what?"

"Of the water. Rodolfo says, no matter what, I must not go in too deep or the ocean will swallow me in one gulp and I will disappear forever."

"Do not worry. We can just *look* at the ocean. We do not have to get wet. Go to sleep, now." He reached over and squeezed Laurita's hand.

~ ~ ~

The middle of the night arrived sooner than Neftalí expected. When Mamadre woke him, he shivered with cold and felt disoriented. Blankets over their shoulders, Neftalí and Laurita stumbled toward the train, now crowded with the house's possessions. Once aboard, Laurita promptly fell back to sleep. But Neftalí's head buzzed with anticipation and nervousness. Would the ocean be as vast as he imagined? What would it smell like? Was it as gentle as bathwater? Or was Rodolfo right? Could it swallow him in one gulp? Neftalí recalled how, in the forest, just when he thought Father might be different, he had stayed the same. What would happen at the ocean? Would the vacation and the salt air change him?

The train traveled through tunnels, over

bridges, and across the Araucanian landscape. By moonlight, Neftalí saw the flat fields of Labranza, shadowed by the volcano, Mount Llaima. He spotted the silhouette of the ruins of a Spanish fort near Boroa and the high steppes and jagged cliffs of Ranquilco.

At the Imperial River, they transferred to a paddle wheel boat. Neftalí and Laurita huddled on a wooden bench between Mamadre and Father. Neftalí could not see much, except the cushion of fog around them. But as the hours passed and dawn approached, the fog thinned to mist, the mist lifted above them, and the world opened up.

A group of Mapuche Indians sat clustered

together on the foredeck, their heads banded with bright scarves, their bodies motionless and snug beneath their wool ponchos.

Uncle Orlando's words played themselves over in Neftalí's mind. *The Mapuche people have lived here for hundreds of years. Why should they leave their homeland?*

Was this family being forced farther and farther from everything they had ever known?

Neftalí stood up and worked his way toward the front of the boat. For reasons he could not explain, he was drawn toward the Mapuche's colorful ponchos and their silence. A Mapuche boy, with eyes, skin, and shoulder-length hair all the color of dark honey, looked up and nodded to Neftalí. Neftalí nodded back. He found a place near the tip of the bow and looked out, standing as still as the others.

A few moments later, the boy appeared at his side. *"Mari-Mari,"* he said, nodding once.

Neftalí did not recognize those words. Was the boy saying hello? He put both hands out, palms up, and shrugged. The boy smiled and shrugged back. As the river carried them forward, they both turned and looked ahead.

Slowly, the boy swept his hand toward the sky brightening to gray.

Neftalí nodded. In turn, he put his hands

together and then separated them inch by inch, until his arms were outstretched to imitate the horizon of water growing wider.

The boy nodded, then touched his ear. He reached under his poncho, pulled out a harmonica, and began to play.

Neftalí felt the river breathing beneath him, as if keeping time to the slow and sorrowful tune. His heart filled with the beauty and the peacefulness of it all. He felt as if he were on the brink of something magnificent. Did the Mapuche boy feel it, too? Neftalí turned to him and smiled.

The boy lifted the harmonica from his lips,

smiled back, and then continued his song.

The paddle wheels spilled water back into the river. Small waves slapped the sides of the vessel. The weathered boat moaned and creaked. Neftalí inched closer to his new friend.

As their shoulders touched, the riverboat was no longer earthbound. With only the two of them aboard, it lifted into the sky, navigating a sea of white billows. The boy was the figurehead beneath the bowsprit, eyes searching for the way. Neftalí was the paddle wheel, moving them forward as one ancient spirit.

Neftalí blinked to hold back his tears.

In the largest of worlds,

what adventures await

the smallest of ships?

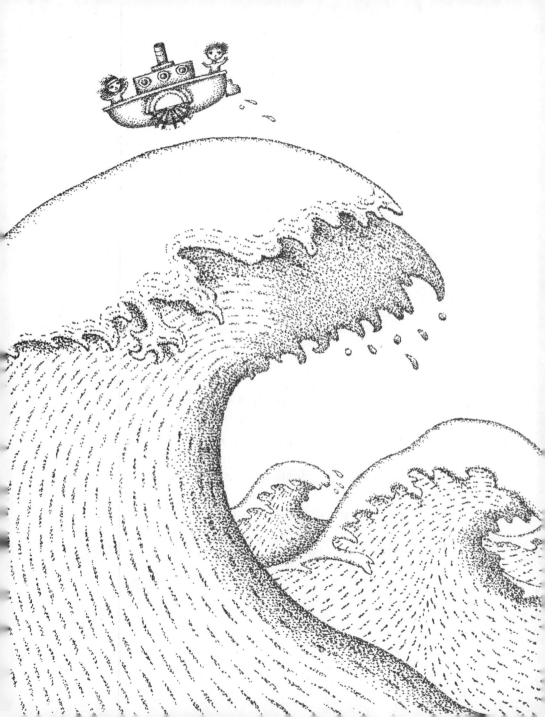

In the blazing sun of morning, the riverboat docked in Puerto Saavedra. Neftalí leaned over the side, watching the deckhands anchor the boat. When he turned back, the Mapuche boy had disappeared. Without him, amid the hustle of passengers preparing to disembark, Neftalí felt alone. He hurried to find Mamadre, Father, and Laurita.

When they crossed the plank to shore, Mamadre guided him to a horse and wagon on the road nearby. Father loaded the wagon with their belongings, and Neftalí searched for the Mapuche boy. But he was lost in the crowd of people.

Neftalí studied each person stepping from the boat, straining to find his friend. Only after the wagon was readied and he had climbed aboard did he catch a glimpse of him. The boy, holding hands with his family, walked away in one direction.

Father slapped the reins and the wagon journeyed in another. Neftalí twisted around hoping for one last gesture.

Hadn't the boy wanted to say good-bye? Hadn't he felt their closeness, too? Had he even looked for Neftalí?

At last, when the group of Mapuche had almost disappeared from Neftalí's sight, he saw the boy tug away from those pulling him along, turn around, and search the scene at the dock.

Frantically, Neftalí waved.

And the boy waved back.

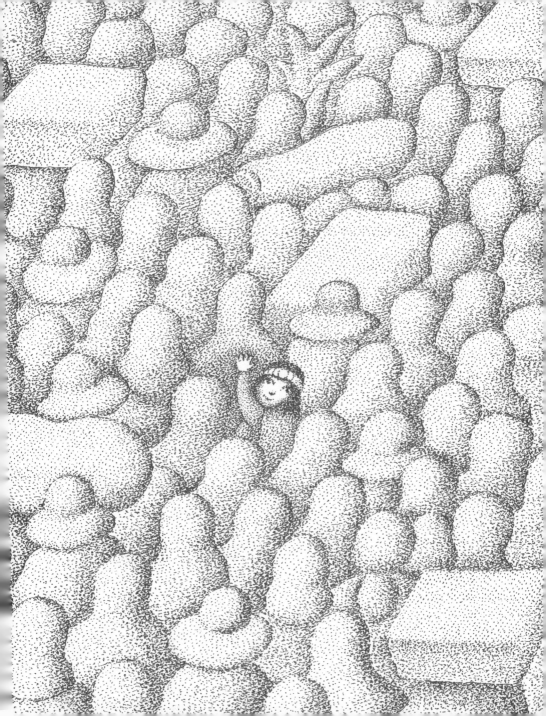

OCEAN

THE HORSE PULLED THE WAGON SLOWLY up a dirt road and stopped in front of several red-roofed houses that overlooked the river. Father pointed to one of them before helping Mamadre from the wagon.

"Where is the ocean?" asked Laurita.

"Very close. We are near the mouth of the river that runs into the sea." Father pointed behind the houses to the top of a hill. "Just on the other side is the great Pacific. Listen."

Neftalí heard a shushing sound, rising and falling, like the snore of a giant.

"Can we go s-see?" asked Neftalí.

"Just to the ridge," said Father, lifting Laurita to the ground. "Then we must all unload the wagon."

Neftalí ran past the house and up the hill, followed by Laurita. At the top, between the cliffs of Huilque and Maule, they stopped.

Neftalí's breath caught in his throat at the sight of the infinite colors and the gentle curve of the faraway horizon. He had never imagined the height of the white spray breaking against the rocks, the dark sand, or the air that whispered of fish and salt. He stood, captivated, feeling small and insignificant, and at the same time as if he belonged to something much grander. Laurita leaned into Neftalí's side. The wind whipped their hair.

Then, at the sound of the conductor's whistle, they ran back down the hill.

Father stood next to the wagon and patted his chest. "The salt air is invigorating, yes?"

Neftalí and Laurita nodded.

Mamadre handed the children boxes to carry, and they raced to see who could be the first to reach the house.

On their way back to the wagon, they passed Father, who seemed to have the strength of three men as he carried one of the mattresses.

Neftalí stopped and grabbed Laurita's arm. "Did you hear him whistling a tune?"

"I couldn't be sure," said Laurita.

But Neftalí *was* sure. And he grinned.

By late morning, they had set up their temporary home. Before Neftalí or Laurita could begin to beg to go down to the ocean, Father came to find them. "Put on your swimming suits. We are going to the beach. We have much to do there."

Neftalí grabbed Laurita's hand and jumped up and down. He *did* have much to do there: building sand towers, collecting shells, and searching for driftwood.

Mamadre smiled and led them to the bedroom. While Neftalí changed, he could not contain his joy. This place, it seemed, was already making Father more good-natured. Maybe *here* Neftalí could share his discoveries with Father. And maybe here he would listen.

On the walk to the beach, Neftalí ran ahead of the family, then turned to look at them. Mamadre released her confining bun, and her hair flowed behind her like a young girl's. Father had rolled up his pant legs in order to stroll barefoot in the sand. He had slung several small blankets over one arm, and in the crook of the other, a basket. Laurita skipped circles around him, seemingly without fear of a reprimand. Was this the same family he lived with in Temuco?

Neftalí raced back to them and took Mamadre's hand. Father began to whistle again, and Neftalí did the same.

With every step, the sound of the ocean grew louder. Soon Neftalí could not hear Father's whistling or his own. What had been a gentle shushing on the other side of the hill was now a deafening repetitive rumble.

POME
Shwahhhhhh

Thissssssssssss

POME
Shwahhhhhh

Thisssssssssssss

Shwahhhhhh

Thissssssssssss

Shwahhhhhh

Thissssssssssss

POME
Shwahhhhhh

Thisssssssssssss

As Mamadre set up their picnic, Neftalí stood and stared at the sea as if he were the entire audience watching a performance on a grand stage. He loved the way the waves bowed to him. He loved the way the sea foam danced in and out, unable to make up its mind about whether to stay or go.

He felt Laurita tugging on his arm. "Look! A stone that looks like a calico cat." She bent to pick it up.

Neftalí rushed to the hem of the sea. "Here, Laurita! The home of a m-mollusk. And a tiny bird skeleton. Just like in the almanac at school."

She ran toward him. "Let me see!"

They examined each other's discoveries. Then Laurita ran to a rocky pool. "What is this, Neftalí?" She held up a knot of string with something shiny embedded inside.

He hurried to her side. "Laurita, p-put it down. That is d-dangerous. It was cut from a fisherman's pole. Rodolfo showed me at the river once. Inside is a sharp hook that can make you b-bleed with one touch."

Her eyes widened. She set it on top of a rock and ran off to collect shells.

Neftalí looked at the expanse of clean, damp sand. He picked up a stick and began writing his name. But he could not stop with only *his* name.

He wrote *Laurita, Mamadre, Father, Rodolfo, Uncle Orlan . . .*

"Neftalí! Neftalí! Neftalí! Neftalí!"

When he looked up, Father stood with his hands on his hips, Laurita obediently at his side. How long had Father been calling his name? Neftalí quickly dropped the stick.

"Is your mind so muddled that you cannot hear me when I stand so close? You need to pay attention."

Neftalí looked at the sand. "Yes, Father. I was just p-practicing my writing."

Father didn't even glance at the words in the sand. "Follow me. We have work to do." He marched toward the ocean.

As they walked behind Father, Neftalí turned to Laurita and asked, "What work?"

She shrugged.

Father stopped before his feet touched the water. He cleared his throat as if to make an announcement. "You will master something useful this summer. The ocean will increase your leg muscles. And when you are in the water, you will be able to think of nothing else. You will focus. This is exactly what you need, Neftalí. And, Laurita, you are becoming far too much like your brother. With any luck, the exercise will build your appetites and make you stronger.

Into the water. Both of you."

Neftalí looked at the immense ocean. He looked at tiny Laurita innocently holding a handful of shells. Could Father possibly mean that *they* should go into the ocean, without him? Even the small waves were choppy, and farther out, the swells rose higher than their heads.

Neftalí looked at Father. "N-n-n-no."

Father smiled, rubbing his hands together.

Neftalí felt sick. So this was his big plan.

"We will do this every day," Father said. "It will make you strong. And if you do not wade out far enough, I will make you stay in longer. Go into the water and swim until I blow the whistle." His voice turned stern. "Now!"

Reluctantly, Neftalí took Laurita's hand. Rodolfo had taught Neftalí to swim in the river pools near home, but the ocean was much fiercer. And Laurita was just a beginner. As they walked slowly toward the waves, Neftalí pulled her close. Every few steps, he looked back at Mamadre, his eyes pleading for a reprieve. Once, he caught her eye, but she quickly lowered her head and pretended to be busy unpacking the lunch. Had she known all along about Father's intentions?

Neftalí and Laurita took baby steps toward the powerful sea, cringing and trembling.

With each step, Laurita clung tighter and

tighter to Neftalí's arm. When the first small waves hit their ankles, they both cried out from the cold. Neftalí turned toward Father, his eyes begging to return to the safety of the beach.

Father only smiled and applauded.

Neftalí knew he had no choice. He pulled Laurita a few steps farther. The water was only knee-deep, but the force and pulse of the ocean made it feel as if it were a monster trying to swallow him. How had Rodolfo known? Had he, too, been forced to endure the waves? Would they be swallowed in one gulp and pulled to their deaths?

Waves slapped their thighs and Laurita stumbled.

Neftalí gripped her hand. "Hold on t-t-t-t-tight!"

A wave broke against their chests. Laurita slipped under the dark water. Neftalí jerked her up. She choked and sputtered and began to cry.

Neftalí looked back at Father. Surely, *now* they could come in. But Father shot an arm forward and pointed to the waves again.

Neftalí searched for Mamadre on the shore. She stood now, watching them, clutching a towel, her face twisted with worry. Why was *she* not signaling for them to come in? Why was she not yelling *"¡Basta, no más!"*? Enough is enough.

Neftalí faced another swell. This time, the

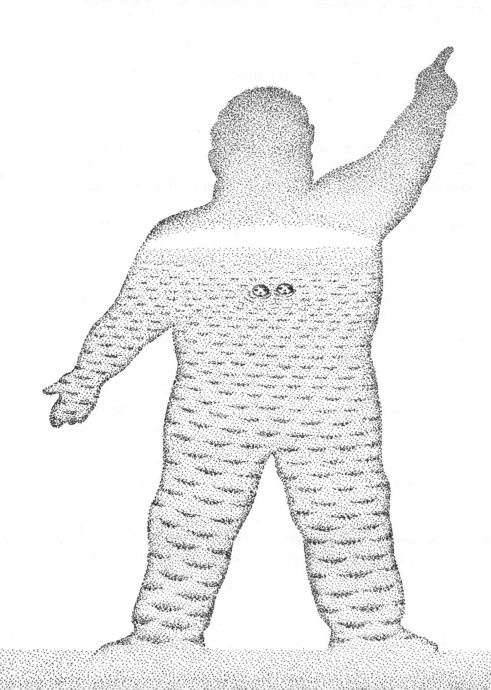

wave was so strong that it pulled him beneath the surface, too. Salt water surged up his nose. He tried to open his eyes underwater, but all he could see was the whiteness of bubbles. He felt Laurita's arm, groping for him. Neftalí's feet found the sand and he jumped up, coughing. He reached for Laurita, pulled her toward him, and lifted her into his arms.

Even though Neftalí had not heard Father's signal to come in, he turned and staggered to shore, holding the hysterical Laurita, who clung to his chest like a frightened kitten.

Mamadre ran forward and took her from him.

Father threw up his arms and shook his head. "Tomorrow you will stay in longer."

Neftalí did not say a word. He wrapped himself in a blanket and trudged toward the summerhouse.

"Neftalí!" called Mamadre.

He did not answer.

Before he was out of earshot, he heard Father say, "Let him go. As long as he is home before sundown, he will be fine. Tramping the dunes will toughen him. *Something* needs to put muscle on his bones."

Neftalí glanced back. Father stood with his arms crossed. Mamadre comforted Laurita.

Neftalí turned and continued walking away from them. With each step, his thoughts screamed louder. Wasn't he fine just the way he was? How would the daily terror in the ocean make him stronger? What made Father so cruel? And why did Mamadre do nothing to stop him? *Was* she just a servant to Father's whims? Were they *all* at his mercy?

Neftalí stormed up the dunes. Something deep and fierce was growing inside him. Where had that feeling come from?

Had the ocean fed it to him?

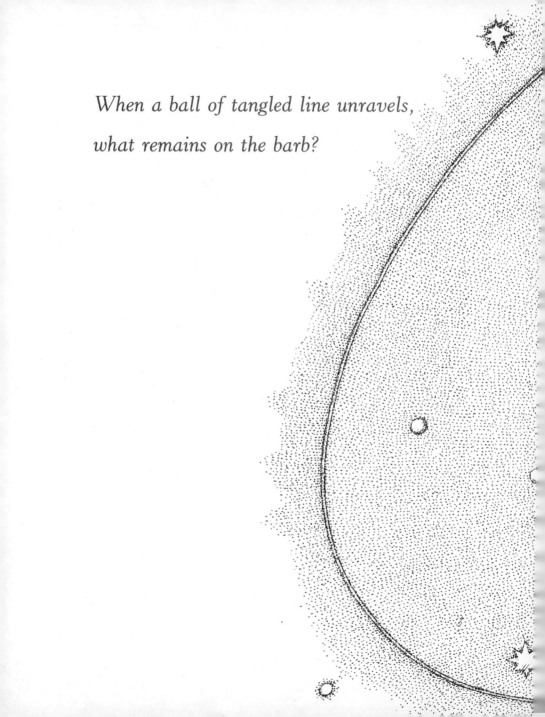

When a ball of tangled line unravels,

what remains on the barb?

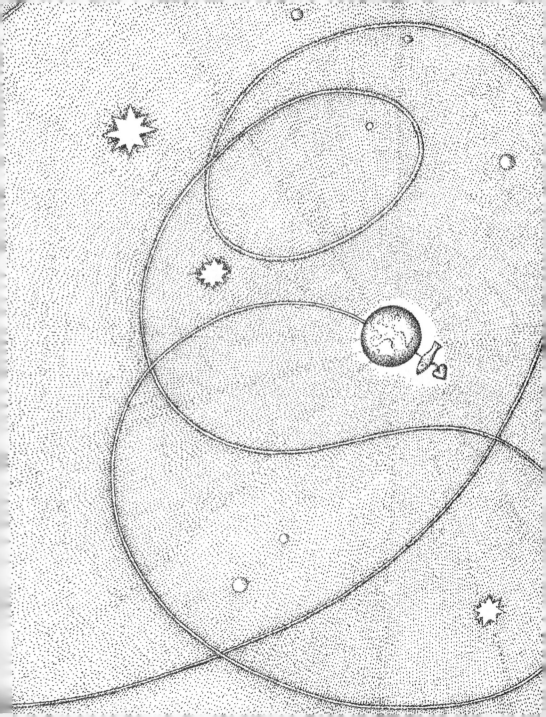

LAGOON

NEFTALÍ WOKE FROM THE SAME nightmare every morning for the next week. Laurita was drowning, and he could not save her because he was drowning, too. The horrible visions plagued him, even as he ate breakfast, put on his swimming suit, and walked to the beach. Neftalí wondered if the beachcombers they passed each morning puzzled over their strange parade: a cheerful whistling man followed by a somber boy, a weeping girl, and a dutiful woman who walked behind as if nothing was wrong.

Neftalí's resentment shadowed him, preventing him from speaking to Mamadre or Father, except to answer their direct questions. His stubbornness came along, too. As soon as the torturous swim in the ocean was over, Neftalí strode back to the house, changed from his swimming suit, and set out on his own. He was determined to do as he pleased.

On a cliff overlooking the ocean, he daydreamed on purpose. He was the flamingo at the edge of the salt marsh, lifting like a giant kite.

He was the banished seagull. He was the swan, whose curious body seemed to slide on a mirror.

When he wasn't daydreaming, he read, on purpose, until he had finished all the books he had brought with him. With the rest of the summer left, he would need to find more.

One afternoon, he walked to the small town and asked a shopkeeper about the location of the library. The shopkeeper pointed him toward a lane that ended at someone's home. Thinking the shopkeeper had misunderstood, Neftalí asked a woman passing on the street. She smiled and pointed to the same house.

As Neftalí stood on the front path,

wondering how a library could be in someone's home, the door was flung open and a bell tied to the doorknob jingled.

A small man, old enough to be Neftalí's grandfather, bounded down the steps. "Come in! Come in!" he called. The man had a beard like Father's, but with much more gray, and eyes that danced. He ushered Neftalí into a small room, where sawdust blanketed the floor. "I am Augusto, the librarian."

Neftalí held out his hand. "I am Neftalí. I am only a v-visitor. For the summer."

Augusto grasped Neftalí's hand in both of his. "It is of no matter. Any time is an auspicious time for books, no?"

Neftalí nodded.

Augusto pulled him closer to the sagging bookshelves. "In what may I interest you? Do you like mystery? Do you like the symphony of language?"

Neftalí smiled and nodded on both accounts.

"Have you already read Jules Verne?"

Neftalí nodded again. "B-but I would read him more than once."

"And do you know the character Buffalo Bill?" asked Augusto.

Neftalí's eyes brightened and then clouded. "Yes, he was a great horseman. But I did not like how he treated the Indians."

"Ah . . . you are a conscientious reader with a taste for adventure. . . ." Augusto stepped to the wall of books. He pulled out two volumes. One appeared to be for a reader much younger than Neftalí and one for someone much older.

"It is never too late for this one," said Augusto, handing him an illustrated picture book of Greek myths. Then he handed him *A Study in Scarlet* by Arthur Conan Doyle. "And it is never too early for this one."

The front door opened and the bell announced another patron.

"Come in! Come in!" said Augusto, leaving

Neftalí with the books.

Neftalí ran his fingers over the covers. His eyes scanned the overstuffed yet cozy room. He did not care that he was squandering good weather by staying indoors. He did not care if reading did not make his leg muscles stronger. He did not care if this pastime did not increase his appetite.

He curled up in a chair and read all afternoon. It wasn't until the sun was low enough to stream through the window and hit him in the eyes that he realized he needed to head back to the summerhouse.

He returned the books to the shelves and then paused in front of a bookcase, his eyes sweeping back and forth over the authors' names:

Hugo

Cervantes

Conan Doyle

Baudelaire

Verne

Tolstoy

Ibsen

Apollinaire

Augusto stood up from his desk where he had been reading and came over to Neftalí. "What is the matter, young man? Do you need help? Why do you look so forlorn?"

Neftalí sighed. "How will I ever read all of these books in one summer?"

Augusto laughed. "There is always time for that which is truly important. If not this summer, then another." He pulled four books off a shelf and held them out to him. "I am only open a few afternoons a week. I hope these will feed you until next time."

Neftalí looked at the books and smiled. "Thank you, but I cannot take them. My father . . . he d-does not like me to read when I could be outside. And in the evening, there is little light in the house."

"Ah. I understand," said Augusto. "I had a father with the same mind." He walked to the window and looked out, then turned back to Neftalí and held up one finger. "What you need is *un escondite*, a hideout."

Neftalí's face brightened.

Augusto signaled for him to come to the window. He pointed outside to a road bordered by trees. "A mile down, there is an abandoned cottage that might serve you." He held the four books out to Neftalí.

"But what if someone c-comes?" said Neftalí.

Although there was no one else in the

room, Augusto cupped a hand around his mouth as if telling a secret. "It belongs to me. But I no longer use it. I live here now" – he swept his arm toward the shelves – "with my neighbors who reside among the pages."

Neftalí bit his lower lip as he considered the offer. He nodded and took the books. "Thank you." He hurried from the house, the bell on the door jingling behind him. Outside, he leaped down the path and then turned to wave to the grinning Augusto at the window.

Alongside the road, the trees eventually gave way to tall sea grass and the grass to rocky dirt and low dunes. Neftalí finally came to a dirt drive. The land sloped downward toward a white-slatted cottage covered in honeysuckle and gone to disrepair. He ran down the path and jumped onto the porch, arriving breathless. *¡Un escondite! His* hideout! Though the windows and doors were boarded and locked, the porch was deep and covered. Near the door, a long wooden box hugged the wall. He lifted the lid to find a few old buckets and garden tools. The books would be safe and dry there. Augusto had been right. This place was perfect.

He circled the small house. Behind it, a burst of color appeared from a mound of poppies: blood red, white, purple, black, and orange, blooming in the midst of an overgrown garden. In the middle of the poppies, an old rowboat went to pieces. Neftalí ran to the landlocked ship, raised his arms above his head, jumped in the air, and claimed it as his own. How could one little piece of earth fill him with such joy?

Beyond the garden, a narrow path stretched toward a lagoon. Neftalí hurried to the water, where two Black-necked swans glided in the middle. As he approached, they turned and paddled toward him, their long necks stretching outward and their bills open in anticipation.

"So then, Mr. and Mrs. Swan . . . someone has treated you as pets, no? And you are expecting a bite of food?"

The swans made hollow wheezing sounds.

"Tomorrow," he promised. "I will be back tomorrow. Of that you can be certain."

As the sun eased toward the horizon, Neftalí headed back to the summerhouse. In the waning light, he ran, his thoughts beating,

My books. My cottage. My swans.
My books. My cottage. My swans.

He couldn't wait to return tomorrow. Now, if only he could keep the cottage a secret.

From what are the walls

of a sanctuary built?

And those of a prison?

The next day, the minute the swim was over, Neftalí hurried back to the summerhouse, changed, and hoped to leave for the cottage before the others arrived. In the rustic kitchen, he quickly stuffed bread into his pockets and scooted out the door, but he came face-to-face with Laurita. He looked behind her to see Mamadre and Father slowly making their way down the hill.

"Why are you back so soon?" he asked. "Don't you usually stay and play on the beach?"

"I was cold and wanted to come home. Where are you going?"

"Just exploring," he said, avoiding her eyes.

"I want to come with you," she pleaded.

"Porfa. It is so boring here. Every day I must go to the market with Mamadre, then I must take a nap, then I must play alone and not make noise while they take coffee. Then – "

Neftalí interrupted her. "Maybe some other time. For now, I am busy." He ran off, glancing over his shoulder to make sure that Laurita had stayed behind. She stood near the house, watching him, her shoulders sagging.

It wasn't any easier the next afternoon. The minute Neftalí left the beach, Laurita ran after him all the way to the house and changed her clothes as quickly as he did. "Neftal-eee," she whined, watching him in the kitchen. "Why do you stuff bread in your pockets? And what is that beneath your shirt?" She lifted his shirttail. "It is your sheep. Where are you taking it? Where are you going? I promise to be good if you take me with you."

He ignored her and pushed out the door, but she followed him.

Abruptly, he turned. "Laurita. Go back!"

As if he had slapped her, she stopped, dropped her head, turned around, and walked back to the house. Her shoulders shook, and Neftalí knew she was crying. Guilt tugged at him. But if he took her, there was the chance she might accidentally tell Mamadre or Father about the cottage and the books. He did not want any of his discoveries to become forbidden. And he didn't want the responsibility of Laurita, either.

By the end of the week, Laurita did not even ask to come along. She just tearfully watched him go.

~ ~ ~

When Neftalí reached the edge of the lagoon, the swans waited. He tossed bread to them and they busily raced for each piece. "I have a secret to tell you. Laurita follows me. I saw her. She does not come to the cottage, though. She only comes to the dirt drive and then goes away. Do not worry. She cannot see much from there.

And she would not betray me on purpose."

Neftalí sat down on the bank. "The morning swim does not get better. When I wake, my stomach is already sick with fear. Laurita cannot swim well, and I worry I will lose her to the greedy waves. I love sitting on the sand and *watching* the sea and collecting what is on the shore. But I do not like that the water is so dark. I cannot see beneath it or how quickly it changes its mind to send me one way or the other. Do you want to know another secret? I always think that I am going to die."

The two swans preened each other's long necks.

"Father *says* I will get stronger, but I do not. And that is making him angrier every day. When I finally come out of the waves, I am shaking and blue from the cold. I even wait to put a blanket over myself so that Father can see my suffering. But it does no good. Mamadre says nothing. Nothing! And that makes *me* angrier. I only talk when I must. I do not even want to be with them. I am happiest when I am here with you."

Neftalí picked up the book that Augusto had lent him the day before. He lay back on the bank and held it above his head. "Now, are you ready to hear a little Victor-Marie Hugo? Listen to this, my friends:

" 'My love flowed e'er for things with wings.

When boy I sought for forest fowl,

And caged them in rude rushes' mesh,

And fed them with my breakfast roll;

So that, though fragile were the door,

They rarely fled, and even then

Would flutter back at faintest call!' "

Neftalí sat up and tossed the remainder of the bread into the lagoon. "I will feed you my breakfast roll and hope that if you ever flee, you, too, will come back to my call."

The swans swam to his offerings and then rushed back for more.

"Do not be greedy," said Neftalí. "And stay in the shadows of the bank. Augusto said that there are hunters who arrive this time of year and would kill you if they could. And for what purpose? To make a powder puff from your down. Or to decorate a silly hat with your long feathers."

Neftalí watched the two mates swimming together as if one were the shadow of the other. "You are best friends, yes? Always together. I am only a little jealous." He leaned back and listened to the waterbirds: the screeches of seagulls, the song of the deep-throated cormorant, and the now-familiar *chirrup chirrup* of the swans.

"My swans, is it true what they say? Do you sing *el canto del cisne*, one last song before you die? No, do not tell me the answer to that. It is something I can live without knowing. Hide in the tall grass, my friends, so the hunters cannot find you."

Neftalí walked back to the cottage and sat on the porch, surveying his summer museum: fish bones, shells, crab claws, sea glass, mother-of-pearl, and the faithful sheep – all arranged on makeshift shelves of old wooden boards stacked on rocks. Contented that everything was in its place, he leaned against the porch post and continued reading.

A few weeks later, when Neftalí reached the edge of the lagoon, he waved his arms. "My friends, I am here! Where are you?" He threw a few pieces of bread in the water, but it turned to mush and sank. He called again and then whistled. The swans did not come. The lagoon was strangely quiet. Even the gulls and cormorants had disappeared.

Neftalí searched the bank, pushing aside the tall grass. He stalked the perimeter of the salt marsh. He tried to convince himself that the swans were safe. Maybe whoever had once fed them had come back. Maybe they were now begging near another property.

He decided to walk to a house in the distance and ask about the swans. He turned up a lane, unsure of where it led. It was there that he saw the trail of blood. A sinking feeling enveloped him. He heard a rustling in the bushes and turned toward it. In the muddy reeds, the male swan wobbled. Blood pooled beneath him. For a moment, Neftalí's stomach felt as if it might erupt and he swayed. But a desperate whine from the swan steadied him.

Neftalí stepped closer and frantically searched for the swan's mate. But she was nowhere.

Gently, he stooped and lifted the enormous

bird that made no attempt to resist. Neftalí struggled to carry him back to the cottage. The swan felt all the heavier because of the weight of Neftalí's heart. He laid the swan on the porch, took a bucket from the storage bench, and fetched water from the lagoon. Then, he blotted the gash with the corner of his shirt. His voice shook. *"Mi cisne, mi cisne.* My swan, my swan, whoever did this to you is a barbarian!" Neftalí stroked the bird's neck. "The hunters killed her, didn't they?" He laid his head on the bird's back. "You must eat or you will die, too." He reached into his pocket and pulled out tiny bits of bread, and gently nudged them between the swan's orange beak.

As the afternoon wore on, Neftalí could not bear the idea of leaving the swan. But if he did not arrive back at the house on time, he couldn't imagine what Father might do or forbid him to do. . . . He stayed with the swan until the sun was nothing more than a dot on the horizon, then he raced back to the summerhouse.

As he approached, he saw Laurita playing outside. She stopped and squinted at him, then pointed at his chest. "What happened, Neftalí? Are you hurt?"

Neftalí looked down. His shirt was covered in blood. He groaned. "No, no. I am fine." Frantically, he looked around. "Where are

Mamadre and Father?"

"Inside. But . . . ?" Laurita continued to point at his bloodied shirt.

"Laurita, it is not my blood. It is the blood of a swan. I need you to help me."

"Help you do what?"

"Can you sneak into the house quickly and bring me a clean shirt?"

She nodded.

"Do not tell Mamadre and Father about the blood."

Laurita hesitated. "I won't tell . . . but . . . only if you take me with you tomorrow."

Neftalí ran his fingers through his hair. "I

will have to ask permission. And Father might say no."

"But if you ask in a polite way . . . "

Neftalí sighed. "Okay, then. Now hurry."

He waited as Laurita skipped into the house. A few minutes later, she returned with a clean shirt. He took off the bloodied one, hid it within a dense bush, and redressed.

As the two walked into the house, Mamadre and Father met them.

"We are sitting down to dinner soon," said Mamadre.

"Wash your hands," said Father.

Acting as if nothing unusual had happened,

Neftalí and Laurita washed their hands together in the sink. Like a conspirator, Laurita caught Neftalí's eye and smiled.

"Thank you," he whispered, praying that Laurita would continue to be sympathetic and not turn into *una chismosa,* a tattletale.

~ ~ ~

The next morning on the beach, as soon as the swim in the ocean was behind them, Neftalí grabbed Laurita's hand and stood in front of Father and Mamadre. "Can Laurita come with me today? There is a flamingo's nest that she would like to see. I p-promise to watch her."

"Be sure she stays close to you," said

Father. "And do not wait so long to return to the house. Last night you were much too late. I do not want to come looking for the two of you."

Neftalí made a mental note to leave the cottage well before sunset.

He held Laurita's hand and walked her calmly to the top of the hill. When they were out of their parents' sight, Laurita pulled her hand from his and jumped up and down.

"Calm down, Laurita, and listen. When we get to the house, change into your clothes, and then find some old rags and a blanket. I will get bread from the kitchen."

"What are they for?"

"I will explain everything when we are on our way. Right now, we must hurry."

~ ~ ~

While they walked on the road toward the cottage, Neftalí told Laurita everything: about Augusto, the hideout, the lagoon, the swans, and the hunters. Every few moments, Neftalí paused and said, "And you must not tell anyone." Each time, Laurita nodded earnestly. Before they even arrived at the porch or laid eyes on the swan, Laurita wrung her hands and repeated over and over, "*¡Pobrecito, pobrecito!*" Poor thing, poor thing.

Neftalí found the swan as he had left him,

lying in a heap on the porch with his eyes closed.

Laurita hovered over him. "He is not dead, is he?"

Neftalí reached out and stroked his neck. "No, just sleeping."

At his touch, the swan's eyes opened and he trembled, then tried to stand, only to slump back down.

"Do not be frightened, my swan," said Neftalí, his voice smooth and calm. "This is my sister, Laurita. In a few days, when you are better, we will go back to the water. I promise. But for now, you must rest."

Neftalí looked at Laurita, whose eyes were

round and solemn. He nodded toward the bucket. "Bring some water from the lagoon so I can clean him. Then, before we leave, we will fill it with fresh water for him to drink."

Laurita retrieved the bucket and rushed to the lagoon and back.

While Neftalí wiped the blood from the swan's body, Laurita stroked his head as if he were a baby. The bird closed his eyes. "Do not worry," she said. "We are here now. And we will take care of you. Poor, poor thing."

Every day for two weeks, Neftalí and Laurita came to take care of the swan. Laurita brought fresh water and arranged and rearranged the blanket to create a soft nest. Neftalí cleaned his wounds, fed him tiny balls of bread, and encouraged the bird to stand and walk, even though he could only take a few steps before collapsing. And when, at last, the wound healed enough, Neftalí kept his promise.

~ ~ ~

Finally, the day came. Neftalí carried the swan toward the lagoon.

Laurita walked beside him, fretting. "Is he safe? Go slow, Neftalí. Careful."

When they reached the bank's edge, Neftalí lowered the swan to the ground.

"Now what?" asked Laurita.

"We must remind him that his home is in the lagoon." He stood over the swan and carefully dipped his bill into the water. Then Neftalí let go of him. For a moment, the swan stayed on the surface, but then he listed into the water, sinking.

Laurita screamed, "Neftalí! Do something!"

Neftalí lunged for the swan and heaved him into his arms. He fell back on the bank, sat up, and cradled him against his chest. "What is the matter, Mr. Swan?"

Laurita sat down next to them. "Maybe he will feel better if you tell him all that you can see."

Neftalí gave her a tiny smile, recalling the times she had stood at the window for him. He looked out at the lagoon. "I see seagulls standing like soldiers on the sand. In the water, hundreds of flamingos raise their curved beaks. Now they are running and lifting into the wind. Look at them! They form one gigantic creature in the sky, a bird of a thousand wings. What color are they? you ask. The color of a baby's cheek. There is more. I see cliffs that are too steep to climb. And two clouds in a lazy race. Which one will win? I cannot tell."

Laurita looked out over the lagoon, too. "Neftalí, where are the rest of the swans?"

"The hunters must have killed them or frightened them away. When our swan is stronger, we will take him to another spot. Maybe to Lake Budi. There are many swans there."

Laurita put her hands together, in prayer. "He *must* get better."

But even after another week of devoted attention, the swan had made little progress. He seemed to grow weaker and more despondent.

On the day that marked three weeks since he'd found the swan, Neftalí waited at the top of the hill for Laurita to dry off from the morning swim. She finally ran up to him. "I cannot go with you today. Mamadre says I must go with her to visit someone who has a girl my age. But I don't want to play with a girl I do not know.

I want to go with you."

"It is all right, Laurita. One day will not make a difference."

"There was fish left over from dinner last night. I hid it near the back door in some paper. Maybe he will like it. But only give him teeny tiny bites. Don't forget to get fresh water for him. And make sure to shake the blanket and arrange it around him like I do. And . . ."

Neftalí put his hand on her arm. "Laurita, I promise to do everything." Then he hurried away, leaving her wringing her hands with worry.

~ ~ ~

When Neftalí reached the cottage, the swan

lifted his head and made a short, pitiful bleat. "You greet me today, Mr. Swan," said Neftalí. "I hope that is a good sign."

Yet again, he carted the swan to the water. But the weak bird only huddled against the bank, as if wanting to rest. Neftalí lifted him back into his arms. "Do not worry, my swan. Tomorrow is another day." He trudged up the lane. "You will like the fish Laurita sent you. It will make you stronger. She was sad not to come today, but I am sure she will be back tomorrow. And we can bring more fish. It is no trouble. And when you feel a little better, then you will swim in the lagoon again. I will help you. You will see."

Neftalí slowed. "You feel heavier today. Maybe you are gaining weight. That would be a good sign." He walked forward. "We are almost to the cottage. And I will arrange everything as Laurita instructed. She is a bossy nurse, no?"

Above them, a flock of seagulls soared toward the ocean, growing smaller and smaller. "Where are they headed, my friend? Can you tell me what they do so far out over the water?"

A cool wind gusted.

The sea grass whispered.

Neftalí took one short step and then another. "Almost there . . ."

He felt a feathery coolness on his arm.

"Yes, rest your head, my friend. Rest your head. . . ."

The swan's silky neck unfurled. And the life disappeared from his body.

Neftalí kept walking, his arms aching. Tears brimmed in his eyes and spilled over. He stumbled. "N-n-no. N-n-not today. Not any d-d-day," he whimpered.

He reached the porch and sank to the step.

How long had it taken him to arrive at the cottage?

A minute? A month? A year?

~ ~ ~

It was almost sunset when Laurita and

Mamadre found him there, still rocking the swan. Laurita ran to him, sat at his side, put her head on his shoulder, and began to cry.

Neftalí looked up at Mamadre. "It is not t-t-true. It is not t-t-true. His mate was k-k-killed. A hunter beat him. We took care of him. . . . But t-t-today . . ."

Mamadre sat on the other side of Neftalí. With her hand, she wiped his tears. "I know. When you did not come home, Laurita told me. There was nothing more you could have done. He must have been injured on the inside, too."

"His w-w-wounds healed. B-b-but he still seemed s-s-sad."

Mamadre put her arm around Neftalí's shoulder. "Wounds are deceiving. Maybe his pain was from something else. A swan needs other swans, just as people need other people."

Neftalí buried his face in the swan's feathers.

Laurita hiccuped through her tears.

Mamadre stood, took off her shawl, and spread it on the ground. Then, with strength Neftalí did not know she had, Mamadre lifted the swan from his arms, tenderly laid him on the shawl, and folded the fabric over his body. "I will come back with you tomorrow and we will bury your friend. Can you think of a good spot?"

Neftalí nodded. "In the p-p-poppies."

Mamadre pulled Neftalí onto her lap and rocked him, just as he had rocked the swan.

By the time they left the cottage, the sun had disappeared. As they walked home, Neftalí held hands with Mamadre and Laurita. It was dark when they finally reached the edge of the yard. Father's shadowy figure moved in the light of a window.

Neftalí froze and his voice trembled. "Father w-w-will be upset. And it is all m-m-my fault."

Mamadre kneeled in front of them. She put one hand on Neftalí's shoulder and the other on Laurita's. "I will say that I took Laurita for a walk. We met up with you, and the lagoon was so beautiful, *I* decided to stay until sunset. *That* is why we are so late." Mamadre looked from Neftalí to Laurita. "When we go into the house, go straight to your bedroom. I will tell Father you are both much too dirty to join us. I will bring dinner to you, later. Do you understand?"

Neftalí reached out and hugged Mamadre's neck tight. He wanted to tell her how much he loved her. He wanted to tell her he was sorry for being angry with her and not talking to her. But his overwhelming emotions stood in the way of his words.

"There now. Let's go inside," she said.

But Neftalí wasn't ready to let her go. He needed one more moment. He whispered in her ear, "It is not true what they say."

"And what is that, my son?"

A tear ran down his cheek. "Swans do not sing when they die."

~ ~ ~

Summer dwindled. Within a few weeks, the yellow sun changed to gold and the shadows lengthened. But the everlasting waves stayed the same, rushing in and sucking back to sea. Neftalí said good-bye to Augusto, packed away all of his summer treasures, and stayed closer to the summerhouse. He wrote words everywhere: on fence posts, on bleached driftwood, and on the old boats near the shore.

On their last day in Puerto Saavedra, Father stood on the beach with his arms crossed.

Neftalí and Laurita stood in front of him, their fingers entwined.

"You have not tried hard enough, Neftalí. After the entire summer, it looks as if you have grown more frail instead of stronger."

"He has grown taller, that is all," said Mamadre. "And, José, look at the healthy color in his face."

Father ran his hand over his beard, staring at Neftalí. "All I see is your foolishness. You are still obsessive. You have not changed one bit, have you?"

Neftalí stared at the flecks in the sand.

"*I* am a better swimmer," offered Laurita.

Father ignored her and shook his head. "Let us get this over with. In you go."

Neftalí tugged Laurita forward and stepped into the water. His stomach recoiled, his fear as intense as it had been on the first day of summer.

How could he love a place so much and hate it at the same time? How could the water feel as if it were part of something deep inside of him and at the same time seem so foreign?

The water rose. He fought each wave. Thoughts of drowning dragged him down with panic. But when he lost his footing, he did not sink. He kicked his feet, stroked one arm, and pulled Laurita with the other.

"Kick your legs, Laurita, and push the water with your arm!"

During a long lull between waves, he found the sand again and looked out. His eyes blurred, and he lifted a hand to shade them. Beyond the swells, an unlikely regatta appeared before him: his fuzzy sheep bobbing on the water; the Mapuche boy, backstroking and waving; two swans swimming in tandem; Augusto, the happy castaway, floating on a raft of books without a care in the world; and a rowboat filled with radiant poppies.

The next wave crested, Neftalí leaned into it, pulling Laurita with him. Then he searched for the floating parade. But he saw only a blanket of poppies sinking below the surface.

Father was already talking about coming back to Puerto Saavedra next summer and the next one after that. Neftalí did not want to think about how far out he might have to swim when he was older. The next wave pushed him down, separated Neftalí's and Laurita's hands, and deposited him in a roil of white water. He held his breath and righted himself, feeling a strange buoyancy, as if something beneath had kept him afloat.

Frantically, he lunged for Laurita and scooped her into his arms. Neftalí shook, but not from fear. This time, he trembled from teeth-grinding anger.

Father *was* wrong.

He *had* changed.

Neftalí made up his mind. He would come back to Puerto Saavedra. But after today, he would never go into the ocean again, no matter what Father said or did. Neftalí loved the ocean's sound. He loved what the waves delivered. He loved the smell and the taste of the salt air. But that was enough. Holding Laurita tight, he made his way to shore.

Father shook his head, disgusted, and walked off toward the house. Mamadre wrapped Laurita in a blanket and herded her away, too, to prepare for the long trip home.

Without them there, Neftalí lingered. He found a stick and defiantly wrote giant words in the damp sand.

Neftalí dropped the stick, feeling a peculiar sense of ownership. He spread his arms and listened to the ocean's thunderous applause. He bowed. The ocean was now *his* audience.

Father's whistle screeched in the distance.

Neftalí headed away from the beach. A stone caught his eye. He picked it up. It was smooth, pearl-gray, and flat, and shaped like a perfect heart. Nothing he had found all summer was as unique. Neftalí slipped the stone into his pocket. School would start in a few weeks. Maybe he would find the courage to give it to a friend. Maybe even to Blanca.

He ran to the top of the hill and looked down.

The waves rushed in and out.

Little by little, letter by letter, the sea washed the sand clean.

Where will the waves take the debris

abandoned in the freckled sand?

DAYDREAMER

FANATIC

ABSENT-MINDED

DIM-WITTED

I am poetry,

surrounding the dreamer.

Ever present,

I capture the spirit,

enslave

the reluctant pen,

and become

the breath

on the writer's only road.

LOVE

As he walked home from school near the river, Neftalí scribbled in his notebook. He paused every few steps, glancing up to avoid the scattered laundry of autumn leaves on the bank.

"Hey, Shinbone! Wait up!"

Neftalí stopped and turned to see Guillermo following him. He had spent the last several years avoiding the bully. What did he want? Although

Neftalí was now eleven years old, he was still the skinniest and weakest boy in his class. He didn't like to imagine what Guillermo could do to him with one punch. Neftalí tucked his notebook into his pocket, pulled his jacket around him, and hurried away.

"Stop!" yelled Guillermo, holding up a fist.

Neftalí leaped across the damp bank but made the mistake of looking back to determine the distance between the two of them. He slipped, hit the ground, and felt his breath disappear. He sat up and leaned over. Moments passed. Finally, his lungs heaved in and out. When he stood, Guillermo grabbed his arm.

"Are you going to listen to me now, Shinbone?"

Neftalí grimaced and nodded.

"I need a favor." Guillermo's eyes darted to the right and left to see if anyone was near. "All you ever do is write in your notebook. And today, in front of the entire school, a teacher read one of your essays and said you have a gift for words." He put his hand on Neftalí's neck and pulled him closer as if he were a friend. "Listen. I want you to write a letter for me. To a girl. And sign my name."

Puzzled, Neftalí stared at him. Guillermo did not want to punch him? "I d-don't know," he said, shaking his head.

Guillermo held a fist to Neftalí's face.

Writing a letter would be much less painful than a beating. Neftalí nodded. "What do you want me t-to tell her?"

Guillermo threw up his hands. "I do not know. Tell her what girls like to hear. And do not mention this to anyone. Bring me the letter in the morning before school. And, Shinbone, make sure she is impressed." He turned to leave.

"Wait," said Neftalí. "What is the girl's n-name?"

Guillermo looked at the ground and kicked the leaves. "You know her. Blanca."

Blanca?

He watched Guillermo saunter off. Neftalí sank to the riverbank, staring into the water.

His Blanca?

He ran all the way home and burst into the house, grateful for the warmth. Thankfully, no one was due home for a few hours. Mamadre had taken Laurita to play with Valeria. Rodolfo and Father were in town.

Neftalí peeled off his coat and hat and hung them near the warmer, then hurried to his room. He studied the tidy rows of his collections, picked up the heart-shaped stone, and massaged it between his fingers. If only it was anyone but Blanca.

His mind raced. How could he escape Guillermo's demand? He put the stone back into place and shook his head. The letter was inevitable. If he did not deliver, Guillermo would only pursue him until he did. And if it did not impress her, Guillermo would make sure his life was miserable. How should he go about it? He didn't know how to write a love letter. He had never even *read* a love letter. Then he remembered the bundle of postcards and letters in the bottom of the trunk.

Neftalí walked to the salon and kneeled by the trunk, running his fingers over the curved lid, oak straps, and leather handles. When he was younger, Mamadre had made him promise he would never go near it, but he was taller now and strong enough to hold the lid. He peeked out the window to make sure no one was coming, then unclasped the latch and hoisted the top. He inhaled the smell of cedar as he removed the clothes, hats, and the guitar. With care, he lifted out the bundle and untied the ribbon.

All of the cards and letters were from a man named Enrique and addressed to a woman named María. Enrique wrote how he wished María were standing at his side at a castle in a faraway land. How their love was like the rivers that ran beneath the ancient stone bridges he had crossed. And how she was far prettier than any of the women in glamorous dresses he had met.

Enrique's handwriting was elegant, with flourishes and curlicues, and his words were just as fancy. His sentences told of how he could not wait to see María again and were filled with his hopes and dreams for their future together.

Neftalí read every letter and card. And then he read them again. Would he ever be able to write such words? Would the words be so memorable that someone would want to save them? He tied the ribbon around the letters and cards, set them back in the trunk, layered the contents on top, and closed the lid.

All afternoon he sat at his desk, staring at his homework. But he was not thinking about mathematics. He was thinking about love. He wrote the word *amor* on a piece of paper and said it over and over. He folded it and put it in the dresser drawer along with the other words he'd saved. Then he waited. But the drawer did not open, nor did the words arrange themselves into sentimental sentences. Maybe if he practiced by first writing a note of affection to someone in his family, the letter to Blanca would come more easily.

Whom did he love?

He loved Laurita.

He loved Uncle Orlando.

He loved Rodolfo.

He knew he *should* love Father, so he did.

He loved Mamadre. She was the most indisputable. She was the kindest person on his earth.

As Neftalí thought about Mamadre, he felt overwhelmed with gratitude for all that she had done for him. He picked up a pencil and began to write down words that reminded him of her. Soon, his mind tensed with sentences that demanded to be written.

Neftalí took a deep breath and felt a strange satisfaction. He wanted to share the verse. He looked out the window. How much time had passed since he'd arrived home? It must have been hours. He heard voices. Neftalí jumped up and ran to find Mamadre. She sat with Father in the dining room, taking coffee.

Neftalí waited in the doorway until Father signaled for him to come forward. His palms perspired and his hands shook. Finally, he held out the paper.

Father read it, but instead of passing it to Mamadre, he handed it back to Neftalí and said, "Where did you copy this from?"

"I wrote it. I d-did not . . ."

"So, now you are turning into a fool? Someday you will need a job that will put food in your stomach and you will regret this abuse of your time. Back to your studies."

As Neftalí left, he looked at Mamadre. She gave him a tiny, tight smile but said nothing. He would show her the poem when Father was not around.

Back in his room, Neftalí sat and stared at the blank piece of paper that needed to become a letter to Blanca. He stood and paced the room, rubbing his temples. Enrique's love letters to María had been so clear. It was as if Enrique's heart were talking out loud. He wondered what was in Guillermo's heart and shook his head. He did not have a clue. He only knew what was inside his own. Suddenly, Neftalí felt a momentum of words he could not shake. He sat down and began. *Dear Blanca . . .*

He filled the letter with his own feelings – compliments about her beauty and her eyes and her sweet voice. He told how he had admired her from afar and how he was afraid to come forward to speak to her. As he came to the end of the letter, he paused. They were *his* thoughts, *his* words, but reluctantly, he signed Guillermo's name. Blanca would think Neftalí's affection belonged to Guillermo. He rubbed the dull ache in his chest.

~ ~ ~

The next day after school, Neftalí could not bear to watch Guillermo deliver the letter to Blanca or her reaction. What if Blanca threw the letter back in Guillermo's face? Would Guillermo come after him? Briskly, Neftalí headed home through town.

As he walked, he heard footsteps behind him. The letter must have been a failure. His words must have been too sentimental, or not sentimental enough. Father was right. He *was* a fool. Now Guillermo was about to pummel him. His body flooded with the same dread that he had felt before Father had forced him into the sea. Without turning around, Neftalí walked faster.

The footsteps sped up, too. He turned a corner and pressed himself into the hollow of a doorway, his heart hammering.

A few moments later he found himself face-to-face with Blanca.

His stomach flip-flopped, and his cheeks warmed.

"I received a letter today," she said.

He could not look at her. His eyes stayed riveted on the ground.

"It was from Guillermo."

Neftalí thought he might be sick.

"Except Guillermo can barely put two words together. But *you* are capable of such artistry."

Neftalí dared to lift his gaze ever so slightly.

"You wrote it, yes?" said Blanca, biting her lip and twisting her body, slowly, side to side.

Neftalí nodded.

"I knew it. Laurita is always telling Valeria and me that you make the best marks in writing."

Neftalí wished he could shrivel to the size of an insect. He felt light-headed and swiped at the back of his clammy neck. He quickly looked at Blanca and then back down.

Blanca smiled and held out her hand. A quince sat on her palm. "For you," she said. "I liked your words. I would like to read more."

Neftalí took the quince but still could not look at her. He stared only at the yellow, pear-like fruit.

Blanca waited for a response, smoothing the ground with her shoe. "I promise not to tell Guillermo that I know it is you."

Neftalí could not catch his breath. It was hard enough when an adult looked him in the eyes, but a girl – especially *this* girl – made his lungs feel as if they were not large enough for his body. Neftalí's chest swelled with an ache, but this time it filled him with a peculiar happiness.

He turned away from Blanca and hurried

home. He kept pace with the phrase that repeated itself over and over in his mind: *I liked your words. I liked your words. I liked your words.*

Instead of eating the quince, he placed it among his collections. He did not care that it would soon dry and wither. Blanca had touched it. He picked up the heart-shaped stone and moved it next to the quince. Maybe this reminder of her kindness would give Neftalí the same confidence to one day pass his heart to her in return.

~ ~ ~

Each week, Neftalí wrote a letter to Blanca and signed Guillermo's name. From a distance, he watched Guillermo present Blanca with the envelope after school. He watched her smile politely and say thank you. He watched her wait until Guillermo was out of sight and then glance back over her shoulder . . . at Neftalí.

Neftalí waited in the school yard, until he saw her eyes searching for him. Only then did he drop his head and follow her home. She always walked slowly, stopping so he could catch up, and so that she could slip him another quince. But as before, he never said a word. He hurried away to add the quince to his collections.

~ ~ ~

On the afternoon that Blanca gave Neftalí the fifth quince, he arrived at home to find Laurita with her arms folded on the table, her head on top of them, crying. Mamadre sat next to her, stroking her back.

"What is wrong?" asked Neftalí.

"Laurita is sad because Valeria and her family are moving away. Her uncle is ill, and her father must go immediately to take over his business in Antofagasta. Valeria and Blanca will leave with their parents tomorrow on the early train."

Laurita raised her head and sniffled. "Valeria is my very . . . best . . . friend!" Her head dropped back down.

Mamadre stroked her hair. "We will go to the station in the morning to say good-bye.

Let us think of something you can give her to remember you."

"I want her to remember me forever and ever!" cried Laurita.

"I know. I know," said Mamadre. "We will think of something very special."

Neftalí left Mamadre to console Laurita and went to his room. He sat on the edge of his bed and held his stomach. Had someone punched him without his knowing? Antofagasta was in the far north of Chile, about a thousand miles from Temuco. Most likely, he would never see Blanca again. He looked at the quinces lined up in a row, and at the one he held in his hand. Suddenly, he, too, felt desperate to make sure that Blanca would never forget him.

He found the heart-shaped stone in his collections, carried it to the window, and looked out. A wagon rolled by on the street, creating a fog of dust. In the brown haze, it was morning at the station, and he walked toward Blanca. Their eyes met. He wove through the crowd until he reached her and pressed the stone into her hand. She took it from him, overwhelmed, and threw her arms around his neck and kissed him on the cheek. They promised to write to each other every week and forever. Blanca boarded the train, waved to him, and blew kisses to the air. He waved back, until the last speck of the caboose disappeared. Only then did he push his way through the crowd, ignoring everyone's curious glances, even Guillermo's, and walk home.

Neftalí pulled away from the window and turned the stone over and over in his hand. Then he put it in his pocket and waited for morning.

~ ~ ~

Day came. Neftalí dressed and anxiously looked out the window as the scene slowly unfolded on the train platform. The passengers congregated with those who came to see them off. Blanca and her family arrived. Mamadre and Laurita greeted them, as did some of Neftalí's classmates, including Guillermo. Neftalí watched the men gather around Blanca's father, shaking his hand and clapping him on the back. He watched the women kiss Blanca's mother, some adding wrapped bread and sweets to her basket for the trip. Laurita held Valeria's hand. Both little girls wore scarves they had exchanged with each other.

When the train pulled in, the men loaded the family's possessions. At the last moment, before Blanca boarded, Laurita ran up to her, whispered in her ear, and pressed the small stone into her hand. Blanca looked at the stone and lifted her head, searching the crowd. Finally, she gave up and climbed into the train.

Behind a curtain, Neftalí watched the steam rise from the stack of the engine.

He watched as the train slowly chugged away from the station.

He watched until he could no longer see even the shadow of the caboose.

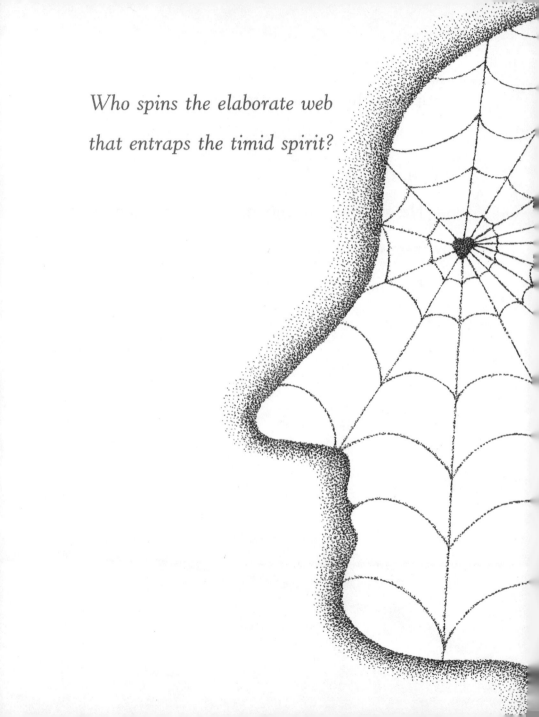

Who spins the elaborate web

that entraps the timid spirit?

PASSION

In Neftalí's bedroom in Temuco, giant deafening raindrops *plipped* and *plopped* and *blooped.*

Mr. Chucao Bird flitted among Neftalí's collections of seedpods and cones, calling out his own name.

A wave broke against the window, and sea foam seeped inside, dribbling down the sill.

Neftalí tried to sleep, but each time he tossed and turned, the noises grew louder. Was he so nervous about tomorrow that he could not control his mind?

He stared into the room. It did not surprise him to see or hear the sound of the ocean, for he had just returned home from his third summer in Puerto Saavedra. And his old friend, the rain, was an eternal resident in Temuco and in his mind. But could it not grant him one night of peace and quiet, especially given his anxiety?

The chucao, on the other hand, startled him. Even though he had been back to the forest many times with Father and had heard the bird, he had only *seen* it that one time when he was eight years old. Now it was in his room. Was it here to warn him of his fate? Had it called on his right side or on his left?

Puzzled, he pulled the blankets over his head and tried to burrow into the mattress. But, even though he was thirteen now and taller than Rodolfo, he was still painfully skinny and barely made an impression on the bed.

Eventually, he gave up on sleep, flung the blanket aside, and allowed the raindrops, the chucao, and the waves their folly. From out of a bookcase, he pulled one of his many books and began to read. But the only sentence that appeared on the page was: *What will tomorrow bring?*

~ ~ ~

The next afternoon, Neftalí paced back and forth on the walkway in front of Uncle Orlando's newspaper office. He ran one hand through his hair and gripped a notebook in the other. Swiping at the clammy perspiration on his brow, he realized he hadn't felt this nervous since he had stood in front of Blanca and accepted the quinces for his letters over two years ago. It did not matter that it was *only* Uncle Orlando he faced. It still meant eye-to-eye contact with someone who would determine his worth.

At least he wasn't facing Father, who still

told everyone that someday Neftalí would be a doctor or a dentist. The more Father insisted, the more Neftalí knew precisely what he would *not* be.

Before he'd left Puerto Saavedra, he had even discussed his growing anxiety with Augusto, who had said, "There is always a way to do what you truly love."

The door swung open. Uncle Orlando poked his head outside. "Neftalí! It *is* you. Why are you walking back and forth in front of my office? Come in."

Neftalí blew out a deep breath. As he entered the office, he tried to imagine Uncle Orlando's reaction to what he wanted to ask. And then he tried to imagine Father's.

Uncle Orlando returned to his desk and sorted papers.

Neftalí took a deep breath.

Uncle Orlando glanced up. "Nephew, you look as if you might faint at any moment. Sit down."

Neftalí sat.

"Why are you so nervous?"

"I want to ask you s-something. Two things."

Uncle Orlando leaned forward, his eyes concerned. "Yes . . ."

"Remember when I was younger and you

said I could work for you someday . . . ?"

Uncle Orlando leaned back in his chair and studied him. "How old are you now? Going on fourteen?"

Neftalí nodded.

"Well . . . you are old enough. It would be a good experience. It would have to be after school, though. And I can pay very little. . . ." He smiled.

"It does not matter," said Neftalí.

Uncle Orlando's face turned serious. "There is one stipulation. We must have your father's permission."

Neftalí's smile disappeared. His shoulders

sagged. "I know."

Slowly, Uncle Orlando nodded. "Let me think. . . . There will be quite a crowd at the house tonight, yes?"

Neftalí nodded. "Father arrived home from a long trip late last night. Even Rodolfo will be here for a few days."

"José will be in a good mood then. Let me choose an opportune circumstance to ask him if you can work for me. Now, you said you wanted to ask me two things. . . ."

Neftalí held out his notebook. "It is an essay I wrote for a competition between all the classes in the boys' and girls' schools. They will publish the winner in the student newspaper. I must turn it in tomorrow, and I was wondering if you could read it first and give me any advice. . . ."

Uncle Orlando took the notebook. "It is the least I can do for a hopeful employee. I will bring it to you when I come for dinner. I am eager to see Rodolfo. How does he like his new job in Santiago?"

"I am not sure," said Neftalí. "We don't see him often, and when we do, he does not talk about it much. I m-miss him."

"Such is life. He is a grown man now." His uncle tilted his head toward the door. "I am sure your Mamadre and Laurita need help. Off with you, so I can finish my work. Otherwise I will not have time to read your paper."

As he walked home, Neftalí tried to imagine an opportune circumstance in which Father would give his permission. But he could not think of a single one.

All he could see was an imposing figure in a dark cape, blocking his path.

That night, drink, talk, and food were plentiful. Neftalí watched for Rodolfo, but when he arrived, he formally shook hands with all of the other businessmen and then huddled with them on one side of the room. Wearing their dark suits, with their heads nodding up and down, they looked like a crowd of black-winged vultures.

At last, Neftalí caught Rodolfo's eye. He raised his hand in greeting. His brother nodded in return, but then turned back to the men.

When everyone was seated at the table, Father pointed to the only empty chair, the one next to Neftalí. "Where is Orlando?"

"He sent word that he was detained," said Mamadre.

Disappointment squeezed at Neftalí. He took tiny sips of his soup. What if Uncle Orlando had not liked his essay? He picked at his roasted chicken, taking only a few bites. If his uncle had not liked his essay, would he think him worthy of working for him? Would he even attempt to ask Father's permission? By the time the guests pushed back from the meal and Mamadre went to the kitchen for the dessert, Neftalí was convinced that Uncle Orlando wasn't coming at all.

Finally, he heard a double knock at the door, and a few moments later, Uncle Orlando appeared. Neftalí felt relieved, but at the same time, every muscle of his body tightened.

Uncle Orlando nodded to everyone. "My apologies for my late arrival, but I have been putting the newspaper to bed."

"Tell us the news," said a shopkeeper. "And we will spread it before the paper is in the hands of one person."

Everyone laughed.

"It is the usual," said Uncle Orlando. "The weather. Marriages. Deaths. Another Mapuche man was murdered for refusing to leave his land. To some of you that is not news because you were involved, even indirectly, with such inhumane actions. But enough of that for now. One bit of news. A new group has formed that will speak on behalf of the Mapuche at town meetings."

"Ah. Supporting the voice of the oppressed. How quaint," said the shopkeeper. "The developers build more businesses, which create more jobs. And you complain about a few

Mapuche who are trespassing."

"On their own land," said Uncle Orlando.

"That is disputable," said the shopkeeper.

Neftalí fretted. Would this be the beginning of another argument?

Uncle Orlando took a step forward and opened his mouth to speak again, but then he stopped, as if he'd remembered something. He smiled at the shopkeeper. "Tonight I am not in the mood to fight. But only for tonight. Instead, with your permission, I would like you all to be privy to an article that will appear in the paper tomorrow."

A gentle murmur of expectancy traveled

around the table.

When all eyes were upon him, Uncle Orlando cleared his throat and began to read, "Enthusiasm and Perseverance . . ."

Neftalí's eyes grew wide. Had he heard correctly? That was the title of *his* essay. His stomach felt as if rocks tumbled inside. He looked around the table as Uncle Orlando read his words about the importance of following dreams and staying determined. He watched everyone's eyes paying rapt attention as they heard about famous explorers who forged ahead into new worlds and conquered obstacles.

Uncle Orlando continued with conviction

in his voice as he read Neftalí's premise that these voyagers were the heroes of resolve and perseverance.

As Uncle Orlando neared the end of the article, his voice became softer and slower. He ended on one somber and thoughtful note: "'Examples such as those of Columbus and Marconi and so many others should not be discarded, because they lead to a more honorable life, and without them it is impossible to live.'"

There was a pause. And silence. Neftalí hung his head. They must not have liked it.

Suddenly, everyone applauded. Neftalí looked from person to person at the appreciation in their eyes. Even Father was clapping and smiling.

"Tell us," said one of the guests, "who wrote this?"

Neftalí struggled to control his uneven breathing.

"A young man who is only thirteen years old. Someone I hope will work for me soon." Uncle Orlando swept his arm toward Neftalí. "None other than our own Neftalí Reyes."

"*¡Felicitaciones!*" exclaimed Laurita.

"Yes, congratulations," said the shopkeeper. "Quite admirable."

Neftalí's hands shook so much that he clasped them together in his lap. How could he feel so proud yet so filled with fear at the same time?

He glanced up and caught Father looking at him with a tight grimace and squinted eyes.

Neftalí quickly looked back into his plate.

Father cleared his throat and said in a much too cheerful voice, "I am happy you are all so pleased with the entertainment."

Neftalí lifted his eyes. Father did not *look* happy.

"José," said one of the guests, "I had no idea your son had so much talent."

"It is only a hobby," said Father with a quick, dismissive tone. "A frivolity, nothing more. Let us talk of something else."

"He would make a good assistant for me," said Uncle Orlando. "And he could use a job after school, no? To help save for the university."

Father's face reddened with anger. "I will give him an allowance when he goes to the university, *if* he studies for a reputable job."

"But the allowance will not cover *all* of his expenses," said Rodolfo. "This way, Neftalí can buy his own books."

Surprised, Neftalí looked across the table at Rodolfo. He had said nothing to him all evening but was now pleading his case.

"It is out of the question," said Father. "Right now, he needs to spend his spare time on his studies that will guarantee *entrance* to the university."

"He earns the best grades in his class . . . ," said Rodolfo. Staring at his little brother, he gave a tiny jerk of his head toward Father, as if encouraging Neftalí to say something. "Isn't that right?"

Neftalí blurted, "Except for mathematics, but I p-p-promise to bring up my score. I would not l-let my marks in school suffer." He could not believe he'd spoken out to Father. Where had the words come from?

Father held up his hand, but before he could say anything, Uncle Orlando said, "University is three years away. I can teach him about the printing press, and he can assist me with the business part of running the newspaper. Everyone needs to know about business, right, Rodolfo?"

Rodolfo nodded. His voice had lost its energy. He said quietly, "As Father says, 'There is always a future in business.' I know that better than anyone."

At that moment, Mamadre entered and slid a platter in front of Father. It was piled with *alfajores,* sweet biscuits filled with caramel jam and dusted with sugar. Everyone at the table eyed the dessert and groaned with anticipation.

"José," said the shopkeeper, "your home is always filled with such interest and delicacies."

"It is settled, then," said Uncle Orlando. "Please pass the lovely *alfajores*."

Father grunted and passed the dessert to the guests. The conversation shifted to compliments about the mouthwatering sweets.

Uncle Orlando nudged Neftalí with his elbow.

Neftalí did not dare look at him or Father. He did glance up at Rodolfo, who gave him the tiniest of smiles. But it was the saddest smile Neftalí had ever seen.

The plate of *alfajores* came his way, and Neftalí concentrated on which biscuit to choose. As he ate, he suddenly wished he could amend his essay to include Uncle Orlando and Rodolfo in his list of heroes.

~ ~ ~

Neftalí began working for Uncle Orlando the next afternoon.

After two months, he mastered the printing press. His fingers were stained black with ink and his apron was soiled from pulling the warm, damp papers off the machine. Its determined song became embedded in his mind:

clickety-CLACK, phew-ah

clickety-CLACK, phew-ah

clickety-CLACK, phew-ah

Neftalí heard it even when the press wasn't running: when he sorted the metal type into the printer's drawers, while he ran errands, and even now as he whistled and swept at the end of a long day.

He hoped that another of his essays would appear in the paper soon. Uncle Orlando had promised, but he had been so preoccupied the last few weeks that Neftalí had not bothered him about it again. Besides, he was worried about his uncle's strange behavior: dashing in and out of the office and never saying where he was going; sending Neftalí to deliver letters to one person or another and making him swear not to tell a soul;

meeting people after dark across the street on the corner and in the rain instead of in the office.

clickety-CLACK, phew-ah

clickety-CLACK, phew-ah

The door swung open and Uncle Orlando rushed in. He slammed the door behind him and began to shut windows. His forehead was furrowed and his voice tight. "Neftalí, set up some chairs and put blankets over the windows."

"Why?" asked Neftalí.

"The new group that has become advocates for the Mapuche wants to organize a protest against the developers. They need a place to meet tonight. So I have offered the office. They will be here in a few hours. Maybe the voice of a larger group will do some good. But, Neftalí, no one must know about the meeting."

Neftalí picked up a rag and cleaned his hands. "I understand."

"If the developers find out," said Uncle Orlando, "there is no imagining what they might do. They have already killed so many. . . ."

A thin, winding fear began to worm through Neftalí's mind. "But how will you know that everyone who comes to the meeting is on your side?"

Uncle Orlando unfolded a blanket and

handed it to Neftalí. "You will stand at the window and let me know if anyone suspicious comes inside. And if one of the developers sends a spy" – he shrugged his shoulders – "then that is a chance I must take."

~ ~ ~

After dark, Neftalí stood at the window peeking out from beneath a blanket and keeping a vigilant post. How would he distinguish a developer from a concerned citizen? What would happen if he allowed the wrong person inside? And if he signaled to Uncle Orlando, would there be a confrontation with guns?

It was not as difficult as Neftalí had

imagined. As people crowded inside the small newspaper office, they seemed far more humble than the shopkeepers who had been to his house for dinner. They were not the owners of the shops. They were the clerks. They were not the ranchers. They were the fieldworkers. They were not the politicians. They were the bakers, the seamstresses, and the blacksmiths.

Although Neftalí looked out during the meeting, he heard everything that went on behind him: Uncle Orlando's sincere voice as he talked about the rights of the Mapuche, the plans for a peaceful protest, the common outcry for respect for all humanity. And when the meeting was over and the people filed out, Neftalí saw their hopeful faces as they clasped Uncle Orlando's hands, thanked him, and said good-bye.

After he helped Uncle Orlando put away the chairs, uncover the windows, and lock up the office, they walked together in silence. In his heart, Neftalí still felt the energy that had filled the room earlier. Above him, the stars seemed to pulse. Had the heavens felt the uprising of all the good intentions, too?

When it was time for Uncle Orlando to go in the opposite direction, Neftalí asked, "Will the protest work?"

"It will work if people are not afraid and if

they can find the confidence to do the right thing. But, Nephew, it is far more difficult when the time comes to actually speak out. One moment, people are strong. The next, they are weak. And it is not always their fault." Uncle Orlando turned away. Then, almost as an afterthought, he called back to Neftalí, "Be safe."

Neftalí raised his hand in parting. At that moment, he hoped that when the time came, he could be strong, but he was not convinced.

It was late when he arrived home. Neftalí went to his room. The moon cast a glow upon his rows of sea glass, shells, and insects, now displayed in boxes and crates nailed to the walls.

Twigs, nests, and seedpods sat on the dresser in dutiful parades. He opened the bottom drawer, pulled out the stuffed sheep, and retrieved one of the notebooks he kept buried beneath it. In the moonlight, he could see just enough to capture his sentiments on paper. Then he returned the notebook to the drawer, placed its woolly guardian on top of it, and lay down on his bed.

The words he had written wiggled off the page and escaped from the drawer. The letters stacked themselves, one on top of the other. Their towers reached higher and higher until they stood majestic and tall, surrounding Neftalí in a city of promise.

Then a tiny, conceited word came along.
Like a hungry termite, it began to gnaw on the tall
words, chewing at their foundation, gulping their

pulp, until they swayed, toppled, and collapsed.

All that remained was one fat, satisfied syllable.

~ ~ ~

In the middle of the night, Neftalí woke to Laurita shaking him. "Neftalí! Wake up!"

He sat up in bed, stunned and confused. "What? What is it?"

"A man came to the door. The newspaper office is on fire. . . ."

Neftalí threw on his clothes and ran toward

the front door, but Father blocked his exit and grabbed his arm.

"Neftalí! There is nothing that can be done. Go back to bed."

Neftalí jerked his arm from Father's grasp. He ran to the street to join others already racing to the scene. He looked back and saw Father silhouetted in the doorway. Why wasn't he, too, coming to help?

Neftalí's heart matched the pounding of his feet as he hurtled down the dirt street. When he turned the corner to the main road, he saw the ball of fire rising into the night.

It seemed the entire town was already

in front of the building, some people shouting directions to those who were trying to put out the fire, others with their hands over their mouths in disbelief, and those trying to keep people back from the danger.

Neftalí pushed through the confusion, searching for Uncle Orlando.

At last, he found him standing in the street, bewildered, holding a single printer's drawer in his hands.

Neftalí ran to him.

In a daze, Uncle Orlando held up the drawer. "It was all I could save. I ran in. But it was all I could save."

A brigade formed, and people passed buckets of water up the line. Still, it was a pitiful attempt to squelch the giant flames. Neftalí joined the volunteers, grateful to have something to do with his hands and, at the same time, troubled by the futility of it all.

As the hours wore on toward morning, the flames died down. The spectators drifted back toward their own homes and businesses. Neftalí stayed until all that remained was smoky ash. He stood next to Uncle Orlando in what now looked like the bed of a giant campfire. "Why?" he asked.

Uncle Orlando's voice was slow and

measured. "The developers think I will give up the cause. They think that the townspeople will now panic and worry about their safety and their jobs. In many cases, that will happen, and support will disappear. And then . . . the Mapuche will disappear, pushed farther and farther away."

Neftalí thought about the Mapuche boy he'd met on the riverboat, and how he and his family had gone in one direction while Neftalí and his family had traveled in another.

"It is not fair," said Neftalí. "It is not right. We should call the authorities."

Uncle Orlando seemed eerily calm as he shook his head. "It will do no good."

"It is their responsibility! This was a crime."

"Ah, yes," said Uncle Orlando with a smirk. "Their responsibility."

"Then it is over?" said Neftalí. "The murders of innocent people will continue? Everyone will act as if nothing happened?"

Uncle Orlando stood a little taller. "Neftalí, there is always something that can be done. For now, I will submit, on the outside. But on the inside, they can never make me surrender my true feelings. I will wait. And then I will start again."

"But how? Where?"

"There are editors who will hire me – if not for a newspaper here, then somewhere else. I will start by writing more stories, stories that might make people whisper behind closed doors. Did you know that many whispers can make a very loud noise? Look around. What do you see?"

Neftalí looked at his uncle in disbelief. What was there to see? Everything his uncle had built was now gone. Why was he not fighting mad? Neftalí threw up his arms. "Nothing. I see nothing. The walls are gone. The machines are destroyed. There is nothing left, except one empty drawer. They have won. . . ."

Uncle Orlando held up his hand to

stop Neftalí's ranting. He walked to a mound of smoking ash and kicked it with his boot. Underneath, glowing embers pulsed like a heart. "You are wrong. Just like Mount Llaima, there is always something burning beneath the surface. Sometimes it takes years to erupt. But, eventually, it will. Nephew, they may have silenced *La Mañana*, but they will never silence my pen." He extended his outstretched hand to Neftalí.

Neftalí looked into his uncle's determined face.

He did not see a man defeated by exhaustion. He saw a man ready to fight another day.

He did not see a man covered head to toe

in soot. He saw a man covered in righteousness.

He did not see a man's red and blurry eyes. He saw an intense resolve to speak for those who could not speak for themselves.

Neftalí reached out and gripped his uncle's palm and held it tight. "Nor will they silence mine."

Is fire born of words?

Or are words born of fire?

plip – plip

plip – plip

plop

oip, oip, oip, oip

bloop, bloop, bloop

plip – plip

plop

plip – plip

plip – plip

plop

bloop, bloop, bloop

plip – plip

plop

oip, oip, oip, oip

tin, tin, tin, tin, tin

tin,

tin,

tin,

tin,

tin

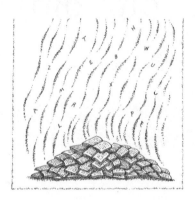

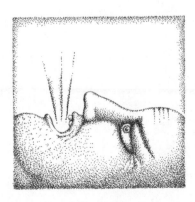

FIRE

"LAURITA!" NEFTALí CALLED from the boys'
school yard. He waved a paper in the air and
then rushed to catch up with her. He handed
her the thin newspaper. "Uncle Orlando's first
edition. Printed in another town. It took him
almost three years but he did it. I cannot wait
to tell him congratulations. And I have my own
big news." Before he continued, he bent to pick

up something shiny from a muddy stream on the side of the road.

"Neftalí, do you not have enough old keys in your collection?"

"Keys unlock doors, Laurita. One can never have too many."

"So tell me your big news," she said.

He pulled a magazine from beneath the books he carried. "I have been made a correspondent for *Claridad,* the magazine published by the students at the university in Santiago."

"But you will not be a student there until the fall."

"That does not matter. Many people

contribute. Look inside. One of my articles has been printed, about the Mapuche. *Claridad* wants more. And they want me to distribute their magazine to students here in Temuco to generate support for their causes in Santiago, so the writers' voices will be heard."

"The voices against the government?" said Laurita. "You know how Father feels about writing against the government. It is risky." She opened the magazine and thumbed through to find Neftalí's article.

"These people are writing about fairness and justice. They are my heroes, Laurita. They write words that stir people's thoughts. They write about changing what is wrong in the world. They are not only students but others, too, poets like Rojas and González Vera, who champion free speech."

"Free speech might get you into trouble." Laurita found his article and scanned to the end. "Neftalí, here by your name it says that you are enrolling in the university to become a *poet*."

"That means nothing. It was just the editor's presumption."

"Neftalí, you should hide this. I do not think Father will like the editor's presumption."

Neftalí sighed. "I am running out of hiding places."

"When you go to the university, *then* you can do as you please."

"I wish that were entirely true," he said. "But I will still have to be secretive about my writing. At least I will be disguised as a student of the French language to become a teacher or a translator" – he lowered his voice to imitate Father's – "'to pave the way into the business world.'"

"So Father has given up on the medical profession?" asked Laurita.

"My math grades." He shrugged. "Father changed my destiny to business. At least I will legitimately be able to read French literature."

"Promise me you will keep up your grades at university, Neftalí, or he will not send you an allowance. You are so skinny. You need to eat."

"Do not worry. I will follow Father's path as long as I can. I promise."

A flock of large birds flew overhead.

Neftalí and Laurita looked up to watch the precision of the beating wings.

"Can you tell if they are ibises or spoon-bills?" asked Laurita.

"No, they are too far away." Neftalí continued to walk, his head tilted back, his eyes upward. When he almost stepped in a huge hole in the street, Laurita grabbed his arm and pulled him to safety. "Look where you are going, not at the birds!"

He steadied himself. "Thank you, Laurita. You know, I am going to miss you when I go to Santiago."

She laughed. "If you can only stay out of trouble until then."

He reached over and ruffled her hair.

"A few months to stay out of trouble is not too much, even for me."

~ ~ ~

A few days later, Neftalí arrived home to find his drawers ransacked and his notebooks strewn all over the floor of his room. Before he could pick them up, Father appeared in the doorway, holding a copy of *Claridad*.

"You are no better than your uncle, inflaming the community." He flipped open the magazine to Neftalí's article and slapped the page. "And what do I read? Not that Neftalí Reyes hopes to become" – his face puffed up and reddened – "anything of consequence. Instead it says you will be nothing more than a lazy thief!"

"It was a m-mistake, that is all."

"It was a *mistake* to ever allow you to work at *any* newspaper," said Father. "I forbid you to abandon the chance of an acceptable profession. And you will not use my money for such a venture. Do you hear me, Neftalí?"

Neftalí looked at the floor.

"It is only due to Mamadre's pleading that I have tolerated this hobby of yours, but my lenience is used up. I have listened to Orlando recite your essays, time and again, at my own table. And when people applaud, it is only out of politeness. Do you know what they are really thinking? They are thinking about what an embarrassment you are to our family. Imagine my *humiliation* when a shopkeeper brought me this article! He says he chooses *not* to come to my home any longer if the entire family is dedicated to this cause."

Father's face flushed with anger. "There

will be no more writing in this house!" He grabbed a notebook and flung it out the window. Loose papers fluttered from inside, as if they were trying to fly. Father flung another notebook and another.

Neftalí heard them slap the porch. Father dashed around the room, grabbing and tossing. *Slap. Slap. Slap.*

Father's cheeks were so bloated with rage that he did not even look like himself. Neftalí backed away from the uncontrollable frenzy, pressing himself against the wall. What would Father throw out the window next? Neftalí himself?

When every notebook was gone, Father marched from the room.

Neftalí sank to his bed and dropped his head into his hands. He hoped that the wind would not abscond with any of his loose pages. He would wait for a while, until he was sure Father was not looking. Then he would collect all of the notebooks and papers and hide them someplace where they could never be found.

Laurita appeared in the doorway, her face pale and her eyes large with fear. She looked at his disheveled room. "Neftalí?"

He looked up. "I guess I could not stay out of trouble for long, after all."

They heard Father's whistle. Two times, three times, and over and over, unstopping.

Laurita walked to the window. "Has he gone mad?"

Neftalí jumped up and rushed to her side.

A plume of smoke drifted upward from the pile of notebooks set on fire in the middle of the street. Neftalí yelled, "No!"

He bolted from his room, through the house, and jumped from the porch to the yard. In several giant bounds, he stood on the edge of the street, hoping to salvage something, anything. But he dared not reach into the flames. Father stood between him and the makeshift bonfire, his eyes wild, his mouth blowing the whistle again and again.

Laurita and Mamadre hurried toward the street. Neighbors peered from windows. Wagon drivers stopped, all watching Neftalí's innermost feelings turn to yellow and orange and blue. His thoughts and cares and affections grew singed and curled. The remnants of his soul floated into the sky like gray snowflakes. His despair and fury about injustice flamed upward and disappeared. And there was nothing he could do.

The whistle blasted and blasted.

Neftalí stood defeated, head and shoulders collapsed.

Finally, Father spat out the whistle and yelled, "*Now* we will see what you become!" Then he stormed into the house.

Neftalí could not move. It was as if all the breath had been sucked from his body.

Dutifully, Mamadre followed Father.

The neighbors went back to their lives.

The wagons rolled in the street again.

Neftalí remained still and dazed until Laurita came and stood next to him.

Without saying a word, they stepped to the pile of ashes.

Neftalí nudged them aside with his boot.

Underneath, a tiny ember blinked.

Where is the heaven of lost stories?

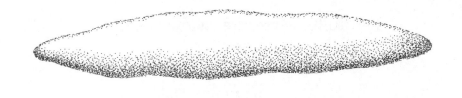

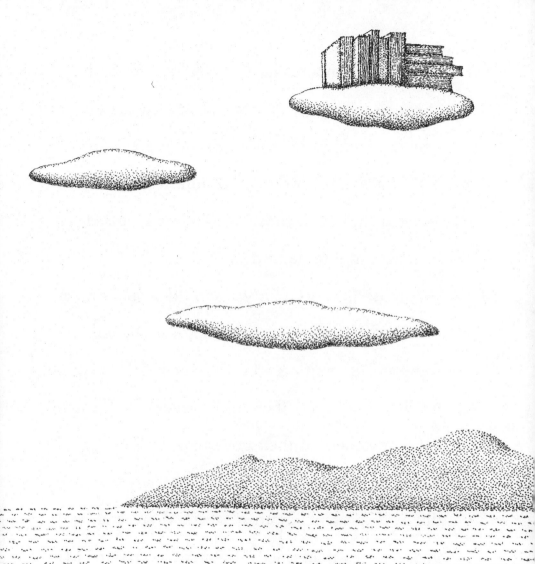

A few months later, Neftalí sat on the edge of his bed. He held a letter he had received earlier that day, telling him of unsettling news. Rojas, one of the poets Neftalí so admired, had been arrested during a student protest and hauled off to prison, where he died.

Grief, uncertainty, and disappointment assaulted Neftalí. How could a government arrest someone for writing what he knew, in his own heart, to be true? Should all writers pass along *only* the beliefs of their government? How could a writer be considered treasonous when all he did was present another view? Were not two views better than one? Was it not better to ask questions of readers and allow them to make up their own minds? He stood and paced, filled with an urgency to respond, to defend, to fight.

He waited until later that night when he was sure that Father was asleep. He sat in his room with the light of a flickering candle casting shadows on his walls and finished a new poem for *Claridad*. Now, he had a dilemma. This poem was to appear next week, not only in the university magazine but simultaneously in a Santiago newspaper. Father knew many people in Santiago, and Neftalí could not take the chance that Father would discover he was disobeying him. Besides that, he could not stop thinking about what Father had said — that he was an embarrassment to the family.

Neftalí sighed and put down his pen. He picked up the local Temuco newspaper and read an article about the works of a Czech writer. To Neftalí, the writer's name seemed unusual and exotic. If only *he* had such a name. He wrote the last name on a small piece of paper. Then he read it out loud, again and again.

He pulled a book of Italian poetry from his shelf and began to thumb through it, stopping at a page to read about a character named Paolo.

"Paolo," he said, but it didn't sound quite right. He translated the name into Spanish and nodded, writing it on the paper next to the other name. The names slid off the paper, marched across the room, and draped themselves on the hook on the back of the bedroom door, becoming a suit of fine clothing.

Neftalí could not resist. He retrieved the suit and tried it on. The pant legs did not need to be hemmed nor the jacket tailored. The fabric was neither too light nor too heavy. The lapels were the width that he liked. The color was soft enough not to offend, but bright enough to be remembered. The name was not only a perfect solution, it was a perfect fit.

He picked up his pen again. At the end of

his poem, instead of signing Neftalí Reyes, he wrote *Pablo Neruda*. He would use this name to save Father the humiliation of having a son who was a poet. Maybe he would use the name only until he became lost enough to find himself.

Maybe he would even keep the name. It might take him places. After all, it had a rhythm like a locomotive chugging uphill.

PABLO NERUDA

PABLO NERUDA

PABLO NERUDA

Does a metamorphosis begin

from the outside in?

Or from the inside out?

The following morning, he slowly packed his belongings into a metal trunk: clothes, books, pens, and, of course, something for which he would never be too old, his sheep. He carefully sorted his collections into several storage boxes, taking one box with him and taking the other to Laurita's room for safekeeping.

He stood in her doorway and handed her the box. "Do not let it go up in flames."

She smiled. "I will guard it with my life. Now, do not say good-bye to me yet. Mamadre and I are walking you to the station. And hurry. It is time to leave. Did someone come for your trunk?"

He nodded. "Everything is ready."

Father waited at the door, his dark cape folded over his arm.

Neither had spoken to the other since the incident with the notebooks.

Father handed him the cape. "I no longer wear it. And you will need it. Stay focused on your studies, Neftalí."

Taking the cape, he recalled how Father had worn it on that first day they had traveled together on the train into the forest. He looked directly into Father's eyes and became lost in his gaze. Who was inside? Someone mean and hateful? Or someone so controlled by his own past that he dared not allow anyone he loved to control their own future?

"Good-bye, Neftalí." Father gave him a curt nod and a stiff embrace.

"Good-bye, Father," he said. And then he murmured, "Neftalí Reyes will not disappoint you."

With Mamadre on one side of him and Laurita on the other, he walked toward the platform and the hissing train. Before he boarded, Mamadre gave him the blanket she had wrapped around her shoulders – the one she had bought years ago from the fair that sold Mapuche arts and crafts. "To keep you warm. You are still skin and bones." She kissed him on each cheek and hugged him tight.

He returned her embrace. "But I am strong on the inside, just like you."

Then, he wrapped Laurita in his arms and swung her around. "You must still be my emissary and send me all the gossip from Temuco."

She laughed. "I promise I will write to you every week."

The train wheezed.

He stepped aboard.

~ ~ ~

That night and throughout the next day, he rode third class in a car full of peasants. It smelled of damp wool from rain-soaked ponchos and wet feathers from unhappy chickens that had been tucked into baskets. But none of that bothered him because he was headed to a place of culture, a place with more like-minded people, where being a student *and* a poet would not be discouraged.

From the window, he watched as miles of araucaria trees dwindled to a scattered few. Still, when the last piece of forest disappeared and all that was left were stark adobe towns, he felt as if a piece of himself had been left behind, too.

When the train stopped, he gathered his trunk, put on a black, wide-brimmed hat, cloaked himself in Father's cape, and slung Mamadre's blanket over his arm. He stepped down onto the streets of Santiago, to make his way in the world.

~ ~ ~

There, in the obscurity of the big city, his writing was as persistent as the weather. Poetry had laid down its path, and he had no choice but to follow. He wrote no matter what his circumstances: when he lived in rooms that were no larger than a cell; when he had barely enough money to eat, and it was so cold that he worshipped Father's cape and Mamadre's blanket; when he had no friends and pulled deep within himself; when his heart was broken or when he broke another's; when he did not agree with the politics at the university or the politics of his country.

He wrote.

Although he had changed his name, his history came with him, even to his writing. The rhythm of his rain-soaked childhood became a sequence of words. His memories of the under-story of the great forest burst into lyrical phrases, as resinous as the sap of a pinecone, as crisp as the shell of a beetle. Sentences grew long, then pulled up short, taking on the tempo of the waves upon the shore, or swayed gently, like the plaintive song of a lone harmonica. His fury became essays that pointed, stabbed, and burned. His convictions played out with the monotonous determination of a printing press. And his affections became poems, as warm and supple as the wool of a well-loved sheep.

Pablo Neruda's poems tramped through the mud. The fieldworker read his words and said, "His hands have moved the earth as mine have."

His poems knocked at the door of mansions. The wealthy read his words and said, "He has climbed up the same ladder."

His poems sat at the table of the baker, who said, "He knows what I feel while working the bread."

His poems marched on cobblestones. The shopkeeper leaned over his counter and read them to his customers and said, "Do you know him? He is my brother."

The poems became books that people passed from hand to hand.

The books traveled over fences . . .

. . . and bridges . . .

. . . and across borders . . .

. . . soaring from continent to continent . . .

. . . until he had passed thousands of gifts

through a hole in the fence to a multitude of

people in every corner of the world . . .

. . . their wings beating with the same pulse,

their hearts eager to feel all that he could dream.

tin,

tin,

tin,

tin,

tin

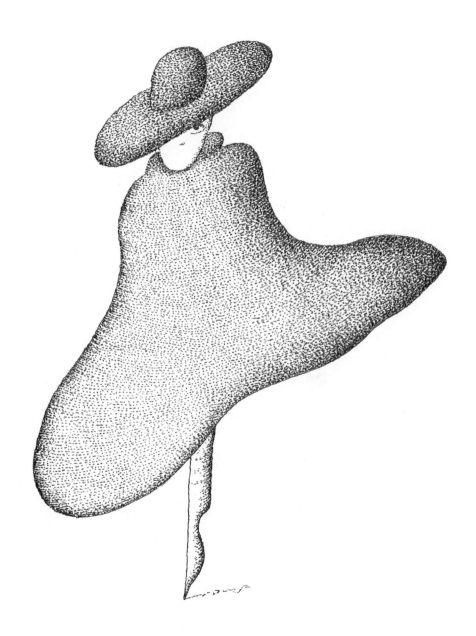

AUTHOR'S NOTE

The Dreamer is a work of fiction based on the events of Pablo Neruda's childhood. The book began with the tiniest intrigue: the incident of the hole in the fence and the exchange of a sheep for a pinecone. That anecdote captivated me and led me to Neruda's essays and memoirs, which led me to his forays into the rain forest and to his trips to the ocean, and to the story of the swan. Which led me to his biographers.

Pablo Neruda (1904–1973) became one of the most important literary poets of the twentieth century, receiving the Nobel Prize for Literature in 1971. If all of his works in all the editions and languages are considered, he is probably the most widely read poet in the world.

Ultimately, his poetry led me. And I discovered *The Book of Questions*. Neruda's spirit of inquiry was contagious and inspired me to create the voice of poetry and the questions in my text. I hope readers will retreat into their own wandering thoughts and imagine answers.

Neruda kept the sheep that was passed to him through the hole in the fence for many years until it was lost in a house fire. After that, even as a man in his fifties, wherever he traveled, he looked into toy-shop windows, hoping to find another sheep that was similar. Although he never found one, he always remembered the circumstance of receiving it and even wrote about it in an essay, "Childhood and Poetry."

Neruda said, "That exchange brought home . . . a precious idea: that all of humanity is somehow together. . . . Just as I once left the pinecone by the fence, I have since left my words on the door of so many people who were unknown to me, people in prison, or hunted, or alone."

Neruda wrote to the common person and about the common thing. He thought that when people touched an object, their fingers left a bit of presence upon it and that a bit of their being was somehow absorbed in the object's memory. He believed that all the stories he ever needed already existed and that their inspiration would be found in the simplest things and the most minute details: in the garden tool, the rolling pin, or the uneven table on which bread was kneaded. Neruda was fascinated by what he called "the permanent mark of humanity on the inside and the outside of all objects."

He said, "It is very appropriate . . . to look deeply into

objects at rest. . . . They exude the touch of man and the earth as a lesson to the tormented poet. . . . The flawed confusion of human beings shows in them . . . the prints of feet and fingers. . . . That is the kind of poetry we should be after, poetry worn away as if by acid, by the labor of hands, impregnated with sweat and smoke, smelling of lilies and urine, splashed by the variety of what we do." Neruda even applied emotion to his pen, preferring to write in green ink, because he thought it was the color of *esperanza* – hope.

His entire life, Neruda collected curious things that appealed to his sense of whimsy, and displayed them: ships in bottles, shells from around the world, the giant figureheads of ships, sea glass, clocks, keys, rare books, glass bottles, nautical instruments, a myriad of treasures from nature, a giant wooden shoe that had once hung over a cobbler's store, and even a carousel horse from a shop in Temuco. He collected people, too, and filled his world with a variety of characters from all walks of life.

Neruda was passionate about love and wrote to express all types of affection: love of another person, love of country, love of humanity, love of common things and beauty. He was equally passionate about despair and often wrote about the mistreatment of others and to announce his political views, which were not always popular.

When the government Neruda supported was overthrown in Chile, by a military government that he did not endorse, he was then considered an enemy of his country. The military regime, led by General Pinochet, established measures against writing or speaking out against the military coup. It was even dangerous to have friends or relatives who did not support Pinochet's government. Thousands of people were killed or imprisoned without trials or were forced to flee the country because they chose to have an opinion different from those in power.

Only a few days before Neruda died, Pinochet's armed guards were ordered to search and ransack his house, as he was by then proclaimed a traitor.

When they arrived, Neruda announced, "Look around – there's only one thing of danger for you here: poetry."

POEMS AND ODES

BY PABLO NERUDA

THE ME-BIRD *(excerpt)*

I am the Pablo bird,
bird of a single feather,
I fly in the clear shadows
and the confused light.
My wings are invisible,
my ears vibrate with sound
as I fly among trees
or underneath tombstones
like a sorrowing umbrella
or a naked sword,
formal as a bow,
or round like a grape.
I fly, I fly unaware
in the hurt of the night . . .
I am the raging bird
in the quiet of the storm.

[Absence and Presence]

Forget About Me *(excerpt)*

Among the things the sea throws up,
let us hunt for the most petrified,
violet claws of crabs,
little skulls of dead fish,
smooth syllables of wood,
small countries of mother-of-pearl;
let us look for what the sea undid
insistently, carelessly,
what it broke up and abandoned,
and left behind for us . . .

. . . Let us look for secret things
somewhere in the world,
on the blue shores of silence
or where the storm has passed,
rampaging like a train.
There the faint signs are left,
coins of time and water,
debris, celestial ash
and the irreplaceable rapture
of sharing in the labor
of solitude and the sand.

[On the Blue Shores of Silence]

Slender-Billed Parakeet

The tree had so many leaves
it was toppling with treasure,
from so much green it blinked
and never closed its eyes.

That's no way to sleep.

But the fluttering foliage
went flying off green and alive,
each bud learned to fly,
and the tree was left naked,
weeping in the winter rain.

[Art of Birds]

Ode to Bicycles *(excerpt)*

I was walking
down
a sizzling road:
the sun popped like
a field of glazing maize,

the earth
was hot,
an infinite circle
with an empty
blue sky overhead.

A few bicycles
passed
me by,
the only
insects
in
that dry
moment of summer,
silent,
swift,
translucent;
they
barely stirred
the air.

[Selected Odes of Pablo Neruda]

I

Why don't the immense airplanes
fly around with their children?

Which yellow bird
fills its nest with lemons?

Why don't they train helicopters
to suck honey from the sunlight?

Where did the full moon leave
its sack of flour tonight?

[The Book of Questions]

XIV

And what did the rubies say
standing before the juice of pomegranates?

Why doesn't Thursday talk itself
into coming after Friday?

Who shouted with glee
when the color blue was born?

Why does the earth grieve
when the violets appear?

[The Book of Questions]

THE FATHER *(excerpt)*

My blunt father comes back
from the trains.
We recognize
in the night
the whistle
of the locomotive

perforating the rain
with a wandering moan,
lament of the night,
and later
the door shivering open.
A rush of wind
came in with my father,
and between footsteps and drafts
the house
shook,
the surprised doors
banged with the dry
bark of pistols,
the staircase groaned,
and a loud voice,
complaining, grumbled
while the wild dark,
the waterfall rain
rumbled on the roofs
and, little by little,
drowned the world. . . .

[The Poetry of Pablo Neruda]

Swan Lake *(excerpt)*

. . . and suddenly,
the lake, its waters hard and hidden,
compacted light, jewel set in a ring of earth.
A black-and-white flying: the swans took flight,
long necks of night, feet of red leather,
and a placid snow flying over the world.

Oh, the flight from the mirroring water,
a thousand bodies aimed at a beautiful stillness
like the transparent permanence of the lake.
Suddenly, all was racing over the water,
movement, sound, towers of the full moon,
and then, wild wings, which out of the whirlwind
turned into order, flight, realized vastness,
and then absence, a white shivering in the void.

[The Poetry of Pablo Neruda]

SHYNESS

I scarcely knew, by myself, that I existed,
that I'd be able to be, and go on being.
I was afraid of that, of life itself.
I didn't want to be seen,
I didn't want my existence to be known.
I became pallid, thin, and absentminded.
I didn't want to speak so that nobody
would recognize my voice, I didn't want
to see so that nobody would see me.
Walking, I pressed myself against the wall
like a shadow slipping away. . . .

[The Poetry of Pablo Neruda]

ODE TO THE LIZARD

On the sand
a
lizard
with a sandy tail.
Beneath
a leaf,
a leaflike
head.

From what planet,
from what
cold green ember
did you fall?
From the moon?
From frozen space?
Or from
the emerald
did your color
climb the vine?

On a rotting
tree trunk
you are
a living
shoot,

arrow
of its foliage.
On a stone
you are a stone
with two small, ancient
eyes –
eyes of the stone.
By the
water
you are
silent, slippery
slime.
To
a fly
you are the dart
of an annihilating dragon.

[Selected Odes of Pablo Neruda]

Pastoral

I copy out mountains, rivers, clouds.
I take my pen from my pocket. I note down
a bird in its rising
or a spider in its little silkworks.
Nothing else crosses my mind. I am air,
clear air, where the wheat is waving,
where a bird's flight moves me, the uncertain
fall of a leaf, the globular
eye of a fish unmoving in the lake,
the statues sailing in the clouds,
the intricate variations of the rain.

Nothing else crosses my mind except
the transparency of summer. I sing only of the wind,
and history passes in its carriage,
collecting its shrouds and medals,
and passes, and all I feel is rivers.
I stay alone with the spring.

[The Poetry of Pablo Neruda]

SOURCES FOR PABLO NERUDA'S POETRY AND ODES

ACKNOWLEDGMENTS

Thank you to author and illustrator Jon J Muth for first telling me the story of the hole in the fence. I am indebted to the Ministry of Education in Chile and especially to Carole Cummings for the doors she opened for me on my trip to Chile. To the many Neruda biographers and translators of his work, particularly Adam Feinstein, Alastair Reid, Volodia Teitelboim, and Margarita Aguirre, her work read from the original Spanish.

Thank you to the uncommon people in my life: my editor, Tracy Mack, who persuaded the text to its fullest in the most enlightening ways; David Saylor, whose vision brought me to this version of the text; to designer, Charles Kreloff, for beautiful bookmaking; to Brian Selznick, for his patient ear and thoughtful comments; to Jim, for understanding the life of a writer; and especially to Peter Sís, for saying yes and bringing his unparalleled magic to the page.

LIBRARY OF CONGRESS CATALOGING-IN-PUBLICATION DATA
Ryan, Pam Muñoz.
The Dreamer / by Pam Muñoz Ryan ; [illustrations by Peter Sís]. — 1st ed.   p. cm.
Summary: A fictionalized biography of the Nobel Prize–winning poet Pablo
Neruda, who grew up a painfully shy child, ridiculed by his overbearing father,
but who became one of the most widely read poets in the world.
Includes bibliographical references.
ISBN-13: 978-0-439-26970-4 (alk. paper)
ISBN-10: 0-439-26970-9 (alk. paper)
1. Neruda, Pablo, 1904-1973—Childhood and youth—Juvenile fiction. [1.
Neruda, Pablo, 1904-1973—Childhood and youth—Fiction. 2. Authors,
Chilean—Fiction. 3. Chile—History—1824-1920—Fiction. 4. Chile—History—1920-
1970—Fiction.]
I. Sís, Peter, ill. II. Title.   PZ7.R9553Ne 2010   [Fic]—dc22 2009010274

10 9 8 7 6 5   11 12 13 14
Printed in the U.S.A.
First edition, April 2010

Book design by David Saylor and Charles Kreloff

I AM POETRY

BY PAM MUÑOZ RYAN

I am poetry,
waiting to seize the poet.
I ask the questions
for which all answers
exist.
I choose no one.
I choose every one.
Come closer . . .
. . . if you dare.

I am poetry,
lurking in dappled shadow.
I am the confusion
of root
and gnarled branch.
I am the symmetry
of insect,
leaf,
and a bird's outstretched wings.

I am poetry,
prowling the blue,
tempting my prey
with fish, shell, and sky.
From beneath the eyelids
of the deep, I seek
the unsuspecting heart.
Look.
Look at me.

I am poetry,
surrounding the dreamer.
Ever present,
I capture the spirit,
enslave
the reluctant pen,
and become
the breath
on the writer's only road.